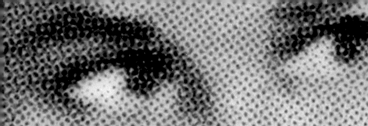

NANCY DREW

girl detective™

Where's Nancy?

D0106577

CAROLYN KEENE

Super Mystery #1

Dropped Signal

George

By this time Bess was looking over at me curiously, the movie on Pause. "Who is it?" she whispered loudly.

"It's Ned," I told her. Then I spoke into the phone again. "Did you try calling her cell?"

"About six times," Ned replied. "It keeps going to voice mail."

That didn't necessarily mean anything. Nancy forgets her cell phone at least as often as she remembers it. And even when she does remember it, half the time it's dead anyway because she forgot to charge it up. "Hmm. So how late is she?"

"Almost forty-five minutes."

"Is that all? Come on, you should know not to worry until she's at least an hour late," I teased. But the joke was only halfhearted. This really was getting a little weird—first Nancy forgets lunch with Bess and me, then she misses a date with Ned on the same day?

NANCY DREW
girl detective™
Super Mystery

#1 Where's Nancy?

Available from Aladdin Paperbacks

NANCY DREW
girl detective ™

Super Mystery #1

Where's Nancy?

Nancy Drew
75 ᵀᴴ
ANNIVERSARY

CAROLYN KEENE

Aladdin Paperbacks

New York   London   Toronto   Sydney

If you purchased this book without a cover, you should be aware that this book is stolen property. It was reported as "unsold and destroyed" to the publisher, and neither the author nor the publisher has received any payment for this "stripped book."

This book is a work of fiction. Any references to historical events, real people, or real locales are used fictitiously. Other names, characters, places, and incidents are the product of the author's imagination, and any resemblance to actual events or locales or persons, living or dead, is entirely coincidental.

❧ ALADDIN PAPERBACKS
An imprint of Simon & Schuster Children's Publishing Division
1230 Avenue of the Americas, New York, NY 10020
Copyright © 2005 by Simon and Schuster, Inc.
All rights reserved, including the right of reproduction in whole or in part in any form.
ALADDIN PAPERBACKS, NANCY DREW, and colophon are registered trademarks of Simon & Schuster, Inc.
NANCY DREW: GIRL DETECTIVE is a trademark of Simon & Schuster, Inc.
Manufactured in the United States of America
First Aladdin Paperbacks edition June 2005
10   9   8
Library of Congress Control Number 2004114472
ISBN-13: 978-1-4169-0034-4
ISBN-10: 1-4169-0034-9

Contents

Nancy No-Show

George

Sometimes **it's not easy** having a friend like Nancy Drew.

Don't get me wrong; Nancy is great. She's loyal, friendly, interesting, and smart. She has a sharp sense of humor and gets along with everybody she meets.

But then there's the mystery thing.

I guess most people have something they do—call it a hobby, an interest, or a passion. For some people that might be painting or gardening or golf. For Nancy, it's solving mysteries. She can sniff out crime and deception from two counties away, and she won't rest until justice is served. I'm sure the reporters at the *River Heights Bugle* have her number on speed dial. And a lot of criminals probably have her picture on their dart boards.

By the way, I'm George Fayne. My real name is Georgia, but nobody calls me that if they value their lives. If you ask me, someone called Georgia sounds like a southern belle in hoop skirts and rouge. That's *so* not me. I'm more of the jeans-and-sneakers persuasion.

Anyway, where was I? Oh, right—Nancy. She's been one of my best friends for as long as I can remember. But I'd be the first to admit that the girl can be a total space cadet. It's strange, too, because when she's on a case, she has total recall for clues, suspects, and motives. So why can't she seem to remember where she parked her car, or to wear two shoes that actually match each other, or to show up to lunch with her friends somewhere almost on time?

I was pondering that last point as I sat in one of the comfortable, wood-paneled booths at the College Diner, drumming my fingers on the graffiti carved in the oak tabletop. It was almost two in the afternoon, the Friday before July Fourth weekend, and the place was almost empty. Summer session classes at the university were knocking off early that day for the holiday weekend, which is why the place was empty except for me, a couple of waitresses, and some giggling high-school kids across the aisle who'd probably just finished a campus tour. Oh, and Bess, who was sitting across from me, paging through the menu for the five millionth time since we'd been sitting there.

Bess Marvin is my cousin, though you'd never guess we were related. She's probably the girliest girl who ever girled. Pink lip gloss, fluffy blond hair, killer wardrobe—the works.

Bess is the type who always looks on the bright side of things. If there's a half-empty glass sitting in front of her, she'll insist it's half full. She's also tenderhearted and thoughtful, the type of girl who would climb a tree to rescue a kitten or help a worm across the sidewalk after a rain. She isn't quick to worry—unless she thinks a friend might be in trouble.

"So where do you think she could be?" she fretted, setting down the menu and twisting her paper napkin between her hands.

See.

I shrugged. Some people might call me pessimistic, but I would disagree. The truth is, I only worry when there's something worth worrying about. And Nancy being late to meet us for lunch—*again*—didn't qualify, as far as I was concerned.

"She's probably still off investigating whatever-the-heck-it-is she thinks she sniffed out over at the university museum," I told Bess. "That's why she wanted to meet here on campus, instead of at one of our usual lunch places, remember? Oh, and that's probably why she forgot to turn on her cell phone,

3

too. As usual." We'd already tried to call her of course. No answer.

"You're probably right." Bess might be a worrier, but she's not stupid. We'd both spent way more hours than we cared to count waiting around for Nancy when she was on a case and lost track of the time. "That e-mail she sent us was kind of mysterious, wasn't it? All she said was something about something suspicious at the museum. Or something. Right?"

"Yeah." To be honest, my mind wasn't really on Nancy's latest case. It was more concerned with whether I had enough cash on me to get a burger, a large order of fries, *and* some onion rings. If I came up short, I could always borrow a few bucks from Bess. I mean, as long as she didn't remember that I already owed her twenty dollars . . .

"She was planning to head over there this morning to investigate," I continued absently, rapidly adding prices in my head. "Said she'd fill us in on the details when she saw us."

"I guess she must be finding something interesting, or she'd be here by now." Bess glanced at her watch with a sigh.

I picked up my menu. My stomach was grumbling even louder than the giggles of those high-school students across the way. Nancy was almost an hour late, and my digestive system was tired of waiting. "Come

4

on," I said. "Let's eat. If she turns up before we're finished, maybe we'll let her have our leftovers."

But she never did turn up. Which was just as well, since neither of us had any leftovers.

After we finished eating and paid the check, we left the restaurant and stood for a moment on the sidewalk, wondering whether we should leave a note with the cashier at the diner just in case Nancy showed after we left. As we stood there, the hot summer sun feeling good after the extreme AC inside the diner, I spotted a familiar face coming our way.

"Look, there's Ned," I said, nudging Bess.

Ned Nickerson has been Nancy's main squeeze practically forever. The two of them are so tight it's a little sickening. He's the kind of guy Bess would call a major hunk—tall, dark, handsome, the works. He also happens to be pretty cool, which is way more important, if you ask me.

"Hey, you two," he said when he reached us. "What are you doing here? Isn't it a little early to start lining up for the parade now?"

He was referring to the Fourth of July parade, scheduled for that Monday, which always runs through campus halfway through its route. River Heights is the kind of place that tends to go a little crazy with the holiday stuff. I mean, the place practically turns itself inside out to celebrate Anvil Day, for

5

Pete's sake, which nobody outside the city limits has ever even heard of.

The Fourth of July is another big favorite, and this year's celebration promised to be even more extravagant than usual since it was the seventy-fifth anniversary of the very first River Heights Independence Day Parade. Various schools, businesses, marching bands, and miscellaneous community groups had been planning their floats and costumes for months.

"Very funny," I replied as Bess giggled at Ned's comment. "But never mind us; what are you doing hanging around this place? I thought classes were cutting out early for the holiday."

"They are," Ned replied. "I just got out of my last one: 'Great Novels of the Early Twentieth Century.'"

"Hmm." I tried not to sound too interested. Ned is studying literature at the university, and he loves to talk about stuff like Hemingway and iambic pentameter and whatever to anyone who cares to listen. Don't get me wrong, the guy is fun to talk to most of the time. Just not when he's discussing *Beowulf.* "Anyway, we were just talking about that girlfriend of yours," I added. "She totally stood us up."

Bess giggled. "Don't be so dramatic, George." She smiled at Ned. "You know our Nancy. She must be too busy with her new case to remember boring stuff like eating."

"What case?" Ned looked curious. "I didn't know she was investigating anything right now."

"We didn't either, until yesterday," Bess told him. "She sent George and me an e-mail about some new mystery she might have uncovered at the museum." She waved one hand gracefully—Bess does everything gracefully—toward the university's small but well-respected museum, located just a couple of blocks from where we were presently standing. "That's all she said about it."

"The museum?" Ned shrugged. "Wonder what that's about. Anyway, Nancy and I are going out to dinner tonight, so I guess I'll hear all about it then." He grinned. "Oh, and I'll make sure to give her a hard time for blowing you guys off."

"Thanks." I grinned back at him. "We'd appreciate that."

That evening Bess and I were in her family's den watching a movie when the phone rang.

"I'll get it," I said immediately. I was glad for the interruption, actually—that's the last time I'm going to let Bess pick the movie without me along. She'd rented some ridiculous mushy romance called *Long-Lost Loves.*

"Hello, Marvin residence," I said into the phone. "How may I direct your call?"

"Hello? Er . . . George? Is that you?"

I recognized Ned's voice, though it sounded oddly tinny. "Hey, what's up? Where are you? You sound funny."

"I'm on a pay phone downtown—I left my cell in the car. Listen, have you talked to Nancy lately?"

I blinked. "What do you mean? I thought you guys were having dinner tonight."

"Yes, I know," Ned said patiently. "But she's a no-show."

"Oh! Yikes. Weird."

By this time Bess was looking over at me curiously, the movie on Pause. "Who is it?" she whispered loudly.

"It's Ned," I told her. Then I spoke into the phone again. "Did you try calling her cell?"

"About six times," Ned replied. "It keeps going to voice mail."

That didn't necessarily mean anything. Nancy forgets her cell phone at least as often as she remembers it. And even when she does remember it, half the time it's dead anyway because she forgot to charge it. "Hmm. So how late is she?"

"Almost forty-five minutes."

"Is that all? Come on, you should know not to worry until she's at least an hour late," I teased. But the joke was only halfhearted. This really was getting

8

a little weird—first Nancy forgets lunch with Bess and me, then she misses a date with Ned on the same day? She can be a flake, but she's usually not *that* bad. "Hey, but if you want, we'll call her house and see what's up. Okay?"

"Okay, thanks. I'd do that myself, but I don't have any more change. Here's the number of this pay phone . . ."

I jotted down the number on a handy magazine. Then I hung up and told Bess what Ned had said. "I'll call and see if her dad or Hannah know where she is," I added, reaching for the phone again.

Bess nodded. "She's probably just running a little late, as usual." There was that glass–half-full attitude again. But I couldn't help noticing that she looked a little concerned.

I punched in Nancy's familiar phone number. It barely rang once before someone on the other end snatched it up. "Nancy?" a slightly breathless man's voice barked. "Is that you?"

"Um, Mr. Drew?" I said. "Hi, it's George."

"George!" Carson Drew sounded unusually glad to hear from me. Not that we don't get along—he's practically a second father to me. Well, make that a third father, after Bess's dad, my uncle Howard. But considering how often I'm over there, it's not like Mr. Drew has much chance to miss me. "I was about to call you," he went on. "Is Nancy with you?"

"I was just about to ask you the same thing." My heart started beating a little faster. Nancy's father sounded worried, and he's not the kind of guy who gets rattled easily. If he was, he wouldn't be able to face down all those bad guys in court—not to mention the other lawyers. Instead, he's the most successful attorney in River Heights. "Ned just called to say she didn't show for their date," I told him.

"Hannah and I haven't seen her since breakfast."

"You mean she hasn't been home all day?" As I said it, I saw Bess's blue eyes widen.

Mr. Drew sighed into the phone. "I'm not sure," he admitted. "I've been out for most of the day, and Hannah was out running errands for most of the afternoon. Nancy might have come in and left again. That's what we're trying to determine."

"Maybe Bess and I can help." I glanced at the TV, which was frozen on the image of a couple dancing in a rainstorm. "We're not doing anything important anyway. We'll be right over."

I filled Bess in on the conversation as we turned off the movie and headed out to my car. "That's so strange," Bess mused as she slid into the passenger seat. "Where could she be?"

"I guess that's the mystery, isn't it?" I smiled

weakly. "Go figure—Nancy disappears just when we need her most. To find herself."

Bess giggled nervously. "Uh-oh," she said. "I guess that means it's up to us to investigate. We can look for clues in her room, or—"

The rest of what she was saying was drowned out as I started the car and the radio burst to life. *"Come one, come all,"* an extremely excited-sounding announcer was saying, *"come down to River Heights for the seventy-fifth annual Independence Day celebration! Join the parade, enjoy food and games, and—"*

I punched the Off button. "Hey, we forgot to call Ned back," I remembered. "Must be the nerves. Do you have your cell on you? I hope he's still there."

Bess nodded and dug her phone out of her purse. As I pulled out onto the quiet, tree-lined street and headed toward Nancy's house, Bess called the number Ned had left. She spoke to him briefly, then hung up.

"He sounded pretty worried when I told him what Nancy's dad said," she told me, tucking the phone back in her purse. "He's going to meet us over there."

I nodded. Ned wasn't the only one who was getting worried.

Where could Nancy be?

★ ★ ★

Bess's finger had hardly left the doorbell when the Drews' front door swung open to reveal the solid, familiar, apron-wearing form of Hannah Gruen. Hannah has been the Drews' housekeeper ever since Nancy's mother died when we were three. She's the one who keeps things running in that household when Mr. Drew is busy with work and Nancy is distracted by her mysteries.

"Come on upstairs, girls," she said in her usual brisk, no-nonsense manner, though there was an extra crease in her broad forehead. "Carson and I just started looking around Nancy's room."

"That's the first thing Nancy would do too," I quipped as Bess and I followed Hannah up the stairs. "Check for clues in the most logical place."

Hannah chuckled, though it sounded a bit forced. "Sounds like she taught you girls well."

Nancy's father smiled at us briefly when we entered Nancy's airy wicker-furniture-and-yellow-wallpaper bedroom. "Thanks for coming, you two," he said. "We're probably worrying for nothing, but . . ."

He didn't bother to finish the sentence. For the next ten minutes or so, the four of us rustled around the room looking for . . . well, I wasn't really sure. Then the doorbell rang again, and Hannah bustled off to answer it, soon returning with Ned at her heels.

"Find anything?" he asked us by way of greeting.

"We found her cell phone, for one thing." I held up the tiny phone. It had been plugged into the charger on her desk, which meant—surprise, surprise—she'd forgotten to take it with her wherever she'd gone.

Bess brushed her blond hair out of her face. "I've been checking her clothes, trying to figure out if she came home to change before your date," she told Ned. "Where were you supposed to meet her, anyway?"

"Vivaldi's," Ned replied, naming a popular restaurant on River Street. "We had reservations."

Bess nodded thoughtfully. "Okay, that place is pretty dressy. So she probably would have worn the blue silk pantsuit, or maybe that new linen dress, or . . ."

While she dug through Nancy's closet and hamper looking for fashion clues, the rest of us huddled and compared notes. But there wasn't much to compare. Basically we were still at square one.

Mr. Drew's face was set into an anxious frown. "All right, enough of this," he said abruptly. "I think it's time I placed a call to Chief McGinnis. Nancy may not be gone long enough to be an official missing person, but the police ought to know what's going on just in case." Without waiting for an answer, he strode out of the room.

Hannah hurried out after Mr. Drew, muttering under her breath about calling the neighbors. I

13

exchanged a glance with Bess and Ned. "I'm sure the chief will be thrilled to hear about this," I whispered.

Despite the rather tense mood in the room, Bess giggled. Chief McGinnis, the head of the River Heights Police Department, isn't exactly Nancy's biggest fan. She's shown him up one too many times by solving the city's latest crime before the chief can get his act together.

"He'll listen to Mr. Drew though," Ned pointed out. "Nancy's father or not, the chief knows that Carson Drew isn't the type to freak out for no good reason."

I gulped, realizing what he'd just said was all too true. Mr. Drew really wasn't the type to panic. If he was worried enough to call the police, maybe it was time for all of us to face the unpleasant truth.

Nancy was missing!

2

Does Not Compute

Bess

Have you ever seen that cute expression a kitten gets when it tumbles off a chair and isn't quite sure what just happened and how it wound up on the floor? That's kind of what George's face looked like when Mr. Drew ran off to call the police. Mine probably looked pretty similar. It seemed to hit us both at the same time that this situation was turning serious. Personally I was still hoping Nancy would walk in any moment now, laughing at our little "investigation" and giving a perfectly logical explanation as to where she'd been all day. But I was having more and more trouble believing that was going to happen.

"This is crazy, Bess," George said to me. "Why would Nancy just up and disappear?"

She sounded almost angry, though I knew it wasn't

15

directed at me. That's George for you; when emotions are running high, her temper often takes over. Me, I usually figure it's easier to just sit back awhile and see what happens next, you know? I mean, why jump to the worst possible conclusions when it's just as easy to look on the bright side?

"Don't blow a gasket, okay?" I told her as soothingly as I could. "We still don't know anything for sure. She has to be somewhere—people don't just disappear."

Poor Ned was standing by Nancy's window tugging at his belt and looking distraught. "I don't know about that, Bess," he said, staring out into the twilight. "People disappear all the time. Just not people we know. Usually."

"He's right." The anger had faded from George's voice, which now took on that clipped, matter-of-fact tone that indicated she was moving into practical mode. "So what are we going to do about it?" She paused for about a tenth of a second, not really giving us a chance to answer. "We're going to find her, that's what!"

Ned shrugged. "Okay. How?"

I wasn't sure what to think of all this. I *was* worried. It *was* weird that Nancy had missed two dates and that her family hadn't seen her all day. But was that really enough to say she was missing and start panicking? Wasn't it just as likely that she had gotten caught up in something and forgotten the date and time? That didn't seem too terribly far-fetched to me. Nancy was a responsible person, but even I, as one of her very best friends in the world, can admit she's pretty absentminded sometimes.

Still, I supposed it wouldn't hurt to start addressing the possibilities, no matter how unlikely. It was better than sitting around worrying.

I sank down onto the edge of the bed, then idly reached up and started twisting a lock of hair around my finger, a habit from childhood that I still fall into sometimes when I'm thinking extra hard. "I think I know what Nancy would do in this type of situation," I mused. "She would start talking about motives, and then listing everything that might be a clue."

"Good point." George nodded briskly, pacing back and forth between Nancy's bed and the doorway. "If we're going to solve this, we have to start thinking like Nancy. So what are our motives? Why would Nancy just disappear?"

We all stood there for a few seconds thinking about it. I'm not ashamed to admit that no brilliant theories were springing to mind.

Finally Ned spoke up tentatively, almost apologetically. "Kidnapping?"

"Maybe." George looked alarmed at the idea. "There are an awful lot of people who don't like her much—like all the criminals and no-goods she's helped put in jail."

"Okay, that's one possibility," I said quickly, before they could start to panic. "But it's not the only one. Maybe she just got involved in something important like, um, I don't know. Oh! Or she ran into a dear old friend and wound up forgetting the time." I smiled, liking the sound of that theory.

George rolled her eyes. "Yeah, right. Next you're going to say maybe she hit her head and got amnesia, right?"

I felt my cheeks flush slightly. How had she known I was just about to suggest that? Okay, maybe it wasn't the most plausible of theories, realistically speaking, but I'd just seen a story like that on a soap opera I'd been following that summer.

"Okay, enough motives," I said. "Maybe we should move on to clues. The first one is her clothes: All the outfits she should have worn to dinner with Ned tonight are still in her closet"—I glanced toward the wicker hamper by the door, wrinkling my nose at the thought of the gorgeous floral-patterned rayon wrap dress I'd helped her pick out last month, which I'd spotted in a wrinkled heap under a bunch of dirty socks—"or in the laundry."

George looked less than impressed with my clothing clue, but she nodded. "Okay," she said. "Anything else?"

"What about that e-mail you guys were talking about before?" Ned suggested. "You thought that had something to do with a mystery—"

"Oh! Right." I stared at George. "What did it say, exactly?"

"I don't remember." She was already heading for Nancy's desk. "But I can find out."

She sat down at Nancy's computer, swept aside the usual clutter of papers and odds and ends that drifted over everything on the desk, and logged on, her fingers racing over the keyboard. George can do just about anything on a computer. She became the official Information Systems Manager for her mom's catering business when she was still in junior high, and she's never met a firewall she couldn't crack. Hacking into a password protected account and finding an old e-mail would be a piece of cake.

"While you're pulling that up, maybe Bess and I should keep searching for more clues in here," Ned suggested, staring anxiously down at the mess beside the computer.

As George bent over the computer screen, I sifted halfheartedly through a stack of books and paperwork on the floor near the closet, feeling a bit guilty for snooping. What were we looking for in Nancy's room, anyway? That was just about the only place we were sure she *wasn't*.

I also couldn't quite shake the feeling that we weren't going about this right. Somehow when Nancy was around, it just seemed to be a lot easier to get started . . .

"How does she do it?" I murmured without realizing I was saying it out loud.

George wasn't paying attention; she was still bent over the computer's keyboard, her dark eyes glittering in the bluish white glow from the screen. "Got it!" she crowed. "I found the e-mail."

"Yay!" I said, cheering up immediately. "Now we're getting somewhere."

I leaned over George's left shoulder while Ned hovered over her right. All three of us were silent for a moment as we read through the e-mail, which was addressed to George and me:

Hi guys! Are we still on for lunch? Is it ok if we meet at the College Diner instead of Susie's place? I need to check out a possible scene of a possible crime at the uni museum in the a.m.—strange things seem to be afoot there; maybe another mystery to track down!?! Anyway, I'll fill you in on the details when I see you. Should know more by then . . . See ya later—

N.

"Well," George said. "That doesn't tell us much, does it?"

Ned stroked his chin thoughtfully. "Scene of a crime," he said. "That kind of makes it sound like a burglary or something, doesn't it?"

"I guess," I said dubiously. "But if there'd been a burglary at the museum this week, wouldn't we have heard about it?"

"Maybe." George was already punching buttons. The e-mail disappeared, replaced after a few seconds by the home page for a local news site. "Okay," she muttered. "Let's try searching on *museum* and *university* and see what we can find . . ."

The machine hummed and blinked, and a few seconds later a page full of headlines popped up. George scrolled through them quickly as Ned and I continued to peer over her shoulders. I read headline after headline: UNIVERSITY MUSEUM OPENS NEW SNACK BAR; LOCAL MUSEUM WINS GRANT; GUARD DOG MAKES DEBUT AT MUSEUM; PRICELESS CHESS SET VISITS UNIVERSITY THANKS TO DONATION FROM SHANNON, CASEY, & STEVENS LAW FIRM . . .

"Check it out," George said, pointing to the last headline. Her voice dripped with disgust. "Sounds like Deirdre's dad is throwing his money around again."

I hid a smile. None of us was crazy about Deirdre

Shannon, whom we'd all known since kindergarten. Her father is probably the second most successful lawyer in River Heights after Mr. Drew, and somehow that gives Deirdre the idea that she's some kind of local royalty. I have to admire her fashion sense—she always looks great—but aside from that, she's really sort of pathetic. Nancy and I tend to ignore her most of the time, but she really rubs George the wrong way.

"Yeah, I heard about that." Ned shrugged. "Shannon's firm is sponsoring a visit from a big traveling exhibit of rare and valuable chess sets from all over the world, including one that's practically priceless—I think it dates back to, like, ancient India or something. The exhibit's supposed to open at the university museum right after the holiday weekend."

"Hmm." George shrugged. "Maybe someone stole that supervaluable chess set in the past couple of days, and Nancy heard about it."

I couldn't help being a little skeptical about that theory. "Um, wouldn't something like that show up on this news site?" I pointed out.

"Not if there's a big hush-hush cover-up!" George's eyes lit up. "Maybe they're holding the chess set for ransom and threatening to blow it up if the museum squawks to the cops. We could call the museum manager at home, see if we can get anything out of her . . ."

Ned looked a little skeptical. "I have a better idea. Can I borrow a phone?"

I grabbed mine out of my purse. That was always easier than convincing George to let anyone else use hers. It's some kind of superfancy one she just bought, with all kinds of extra bells and whistles, and she's a little possessive. "Who are you calling?" I asked as I handed my phone to Ned.

"The paper." Ned was already punching numbers.

I nodded, understanding without further explanation. Ned's father is the publisher of the local newspaper, the *River Heights Bugle*. Nothing happens in town that Mr. Nickerson or his reporters don't hear about.

But the *Bugle* turned out to be another dead end. Nobody knew anything about any kind of theft or other crime at the museum.

"Oh, well," I said with a sigh. "At least we can probably rule out—hey, what are you doing?" I'd just noticed that George was busily typing away at the computer again. The news Web site had disappeared, replaced by Nancy's e-mail in-box.

"Just doing a little snooping," George said, sounding distracted. "Maybe someone e-mailed Nancy a tip about the museum or something. Can't hurt to check, right?"

I felt a little uneasy about invading Nancy's privacy

like that, especially when we didn't even know for sure that she was in any real trouble. But I didn't say anything as George pulled up old and deleted e-mails. Most of them were easy to sift through—messages from the three of us in the room, from her father or other familiar friends and acquaintances.

There was only one from an address none of us recognized. "ZQ underscore, four-two-seven," George said. "Who's that?"

Ned shook his head. "Don't know. What's the message say?"

"Something about helping this ZQ person find a job, I think." George scanned through the e-mail, which was fairly long. "Blah blah blah, thanks for your kind help, giving back to the community after all my troubles, good honest work at last, yada yada." She shrugged. "Sounds like it's just one of her charity cases keeping in touch. Nothing about pilfering paintings or filching artifacts from the museum."

I nodded. Nancy does lots of charity work in the community. It was no surprise that one of the people she'd helped was writing to say thanks. It certainly didn't seem suspicious. That was the trouble—nothing we were finding seemed suspicious at all.

All this time Ned was still slowly sifting through the stuff on Nancy's desk. "Hey, here's her calendar," he commented, pulling out a day planner. It was open to the current week, and a few notes were scrawled here and there in Nancy's distinctive handwriting.

I glanced over the page, noting that the missed lunch and dinner dates were both written down on today's date. George looked over from the computer screen and spotted the same thing.

"Okay, so we can't use the excuse that she got the day wrong or something," she pointed out. "Of course, she might be more likely to remember her plans if she would give up on the low-tech record keeping and buy a handheld . . ."

"What's this?" I pointed to a notation on the square for the following day. The notation read *RHCSoc, 3:00, MHY HLL.*

"Okay, the three o'clock I get," George said, squinting at the cryptic note. "The rest? Who knows?"

Ned flipped the calendar to the following page. "There's something about the parade here," he said, pointing to Monday's date. "It says *'parade, watch then—comm. as cover?'*" He tilted his head to one side, looking puzzled. "What does that mean?"

George sighed loudly, abruptly shoving the calendar away. "It means we make totally hopeless detectives," she exclaimed. "None of this makes any sense at all, and we're getting nowhere fast. Face it, guys. We need Nancy to find Nancy!"

3

Out and About

George

The others stared at me in surprise after my little outburst. Bess had that look on her face that meant I was about to get a well-meaning lecture. Ugh. I hate that look. And it always turns up when I'm least in the mood for it.

"I know this is kind of frustrating, George," Bess began. "But all we can do is—"

I didn't let her finish. "Look, I don't know about you guys." I punched a button to shut down the computer, then pushed back the desk chair and jumped to my feet, almost crashing headlong into Ned. "But I can't deal with sitting around here any longer. Let's get out there and do something, okay? Search her favorite spots, talk to people—*something*.

Because we're not getting any closer to finding her hanging around here."

"Maybe she's right," Ned said, glancing at Bess. "Guess it wouldn't hurt to take a look around town while we think about what else to do."

Bess agreed, and after letting Daddy Drew know what we were doing, we climbed into my car and took off. "Okay," I said, clutching the wheel tightly with both hands. I was already feeling a little better now that we were taking some action. "Where to first?"

Bess leaned forward from the backseat to answer. "What about the Independence Day Festival?" she suggested. "That starts tonight, doesn't it?"

I'd almost forgotten about the festival. Like Monday's parade, the River Street Independence Day Festival had been a local institution for the past seventy-five years. Held on and named after the main drag of River Heights, it ran all weekend long and featured food booths, shopping, sideshow games, music, street performers, and all sorts of other wholesome family-type entertainment.

"Good plan," Ned agreed, checking his watch. "It's still dinnertime, so half the town will probably be there. We can ask around, find out if anyone's seen her lately."

Bess nodded. "Yeah, and almost everyone in River

Heights knows Nancy. If she's been spotted anywhere in town today, we should be able to find out all about it there." Her dimples appeared as she smiled with relief. "This mystery could turn out to be a piece of cake after all!"

What *wasn't* a piece of cake was finding a parking spot anywhere within a ten-block radius of River Street. We ended up settling for a place way over on University Avenue and hiking the rest of the way. If we hadn't all been so worked up about Nancy, it might have been a nice walk. The hot summer day had settled into a pleasant evening, with a breeze blowing in off the river to cool things down.

Okay. Remember how I said it wasn't always easy being friends with someone like Nancy? Well, I just remembered another reason why. Everywhere we turned, people greeted us politely . . . and then inquired after Nancy. It made it pretty easy to conduct our little investigation, but it was sort of disheartening as well. Weren't Bess, Ned, and I real people in our own right? Couldn't anyone see us as anything but Nancy's accessories? I'd never really noticed it before, but it irked me once I did.

After stopping to talk to half a dozen people, all of whom seemed incredibly interested in Nancy's whereabouts but had no idea where she might be, we finally reached the heart of the festival. The three or four central blocks of River Street were packed with some of the city's most popular shops and restaurants, as well as the police station, a couple of banks, and various other businesses. At the moment, the street was closed to traffic, and hundreds of people were milling around, examining the handicrafts displayed in various booths, watching a mime performing in front of Mason's Drugstore, and tasting the creations of at least half a dozen chefs at stands set up along the sidewalks.

"Look, there's Harold." Bess pointed to one of the food stands, where a man wearing spectacles and a happy expression was handing out samples. "Maybe we should go talk to him. He adores Nancy."

We headed over. Harold Safer owns the local cheese shop, and his booth was selling cheese baskets, recipe books, and other cheese-related accessories, as well as giving out free samples of local cheddar, imported Brie, and all kinds of other cheeses I didn't recognize.

"Hey, kids!" Harold greeted us cheerfully, his round face breaking into a big smile as we reached the booth. "Good to see you. Where's Nancy?"

"We're wondering the same thing ourselves actually . . ." Ned quickly ran through the gist of our problem as I popped several of the free cheese samples into my mouth. Rather than seeming worried to hear of Nancy's apparent disappearance,

Harold just smiled more broadly than ever.

"Oh, my. Good one!" he chortled. "The girl detective goes missing. Who can solve the mystery?" He put a solemn hand to his heart. "Why, it sounds like the beginnings of a brilliant play!"

"Yes, well, we'd better be moving along," I said hastily. Other than cheese, one of Harold's main obsessions is Broadway plays. He was already humming under his breath. If he started actually singing, we'd be lucky to break away before midnight.

Bess looked a little sheepish about our hasty retreat, but I could tell Ned was with me. We moved along and lost ourselves in the crowd.

"That was weird," I commented, glancing back over my shoulder. "He didn't even seem worried to hear about Nancy."

Bess rolled her eyes. "Come on, George," she said. "You're not hinting that sweet Harold Safer has some dastardly connection with her disappearance, are you? Get real. He was just being, you know, whimsical."

"Whatever." I really didn't suspect Harold of anything, but I wanted to point out that we couldn't discount anyone just because they were nice, or cheerful, or whimsical. Nancy wouldn't do that. She would let the evidence speak for itself—and we should too.

Before I could express any of that, though, yet another River Heights citizen popped up in front of us asking after Nancy. This time the questioner was Evaline Waters, a long-time friend of Nancy's.

"Oh, dear," Ms. Waters said when we told her what was going on. "I do hope she's all right. Please let me know if there's anything I can do to help."

"Thanks, Ms. Waters." Ned smiled at her gratefully. "I imagine we may be worrying for nothing. She'll probably turn up soon and wonder what all the fuss is about."

"Yes, I expect so." Ms. Waters smiled, the corners of her eyes crinkling pleasantly. "Nancy is—"

A flurry of barking interrupted her, drowning out the rest of her comment. Glancing over my shoulder in irritation, I saw a large, scruffy-looking, brown and white dog of questionable heritage, dragging a slight, elderly man through the crowd. I recognized him right away, even though I'd only met him once or twice. Marcus Pembleton was well-known around town—he'd lived in River Heights all his life, growing up on a ten-acre farm that straddled the city limits. He had once worked his land, producing a variety of fruits and vegetables, but had retired years ago to live frugally but comfortably off a small inheritance and tend to his many odd but valuable collections, from fountain pens to antique garden tools.

"So sorry!" the man called out breathlessly as people scattered before his canine charge. "Oh, my.

Rufus, please slow down! Sorry everyone!"

Ned leaped forward and took hold of the excited dog's leash, managing to calm the beast before it pulled its owner right off his feet. Despite his exuberance, Rufus seemed a friendly sort, and was soon licking Bess's hand and sniffing at my shoes.

Pembleton seemed relieved for the help; he was red-faced and panting. "Thank you, young man!" he exclaimed. Pushing his glasses up on his beaklike nose as he took back the leash of the now-calm dog, he peered up at Ned. "Oh! It's young Ned Nickerson, is it?"

"Hello, Mr. Pembleton," Ned said politely. "It's nice to see you again."

"Likewise, young man, likewise." Pembleton beamed at Ned, then turned the smile to include all of us. "Evaline," he greeted Ms. Waters with a little bow. "Charmed, I'm sure. And girls . . . Why, but isn't there one of you missing?"

I swallowed a sigh. Naturally he was looking for Nancy. Once again we explained our mission. And once again we were met with a shrug and a "sorry, haven't seen her." A moment later Pembleton left us rather abruptly, yanked forward through the crowd by Rufus.

"Oh, dear," Ms. Waters said, watching them go. "I do hope he'll be all right with that dog. He loves animals so, but . . ."

Her voice trailed off. She was too polite to say what I suspected we were all thinking. Pembleton was a huge animal lover and had rescued most of his many pets from the pound, but his training ability left something to be desired. This wasn't the first time any of us had seen him dragged around at the end of a leash by one of his ill-mannered pooches.

"Oh, well," Bess said brightly. "At least he should be able to fix whatever Rufus breaks, right?"

Ned chuckled. "That's looking on the bright side, Bess," he said. "But you're right. Mr. Pembleton definitely has a talent for fixing things."

That was a new one on me. "What do you mean?" I asked curiously. The main thing that had always stuck in my own mind about Pembleton was his well-known—and to me, curious, verging on downright ridiculous—refusal to sell any of the more valuable artifacts from his collections, which could have given him enough money to renovate his old farmhouse and live well for the rest of his life.

Bess shrugged. "He's a wiz at repairing motors and tractors and other mechanical-type things."

That actually meant a lot coming from Bess, who's pretty much of a wiz herself—she has a natural talent when it comes to fiddling with anything from toasters to trucks. Half the time I don't think she even knows the name of the gizmo she's adjusting or the bolt she's tightening, but somehow she just knows how to get whatever-it-is working again. I'm used to it, since I've known her my whole life. But it surprises most people to see this pretty young dimple-faced girl under the hood with a wrench. It's also usually good for a laugh or two. Especially since Bess usually manages to emerge from such Ms. Fix-it moments without a spot of grease or dirt on her outfit or a blond hair out of place.

Ms. Waters was soon pulled away by another friend, and the three of us continued our wandering, which felt rather aimless by now. The hour was growing late and we still didn't know any more than when we'd left Nancy's house. We talked to a few more people, but I was starting to wonder if we were wasting our time.

"Listen," I spoke up as we paused in front of the local psychic's shop. I gestured at the plate-glass window. "We'd have just as much luck going in and asking Lucia to psychically predict where Nancy might be. Nobody here seems to know anything."

"Not so far," Bess admitted. "But maybe if we just ask—Chief McGinnis!"

She was smiling over my shoulder, and I turned to see the police chief standing there. He was dressed in khakis and a polo shirt instead of his work clothes, but his broad, ruddy face wore its usual expression of slightly suspicious placidity.

"Hello," the chief said, though he didn't seem overly thrilled to see us. "Enjoying the festival?"

"Not really," I replied. "We're looking for Nancy."

"Nancy?" Chief McGinnis sighed. "Yes, Carson called me a while ago about that."

I waited for him to go on, but he was already turning his attention to a booth full of pastries nearby. Ned cleared his throat. "Er, any leads yet, sir?" he asked politely.

"Leads?" The chief tore his attention away from the pastries to shoot Ned a dismissive glance. "It's a bit soon to be thinking that way, young man. Of course I can understand Carson's concern—his only daughter, after all—quite natural. But . . ."

I didn't even have to listen to the rest. It was obvious that the chief wasn't the least bit worried about Nancy. It was hard not to feel irked by his casual attitude. He should know as well as anyone that someone like Nancy doesn't just disappear for an entire day with no word to anyone!

Oh, well, I told myself grimly as Bess and Ned made polite small talk with the chief. If the police wouldn't help, that just meant we'd definitely have to get on the ball and find Nancy ourselves.

4

Making Connections

Bess

I **could almost see the** resolve hardening on George's face. She likes to think she's all tough and inscrutable, but I can read her like a book.

At that moment I figured it might be a good idea to get George away from Chief McGinnis before she said something obnoxious and made it even less likely that he'd start looking for Nancy anytime soon.

"Would you excuse us, Chief McGinnis?" I said brightly, flashing him what I hoped was my most disarming and distracting smile. "We have someone. waiting for us over there. So sorry."

I grabbed George by the arm and dragged her off into the crowd. Ned followed.

"What a puffed-up, useless excuse for a cop," George ranted as soon as we were out of earshot.

"Did you hear him? 'It's a bit soon to be thinking that way, young man.' What a dork!"

"Look at it from his point of view," I told her. "For all we know, Nancy's been out of touch for what— ten or twelve hours tops? We aren't even sure ourselves that she's really missing. For all we know, she could be at home right now!"

George glared at me. "Look, can you stop being all Miss Sunnybrook Farm about this? She's missing. Her dad has our cell numbers; he'd call us right away if she turned up."

I bit my lip, admitting she had a point. "Okay, but standing around here worrying or complaining about Chief McGinnis or whatever isn't going to find her," I said. "We need to figure out a plan or something. Find more clues. Something like that."

I couldn't help feeling sort of helpless. The rest of us tend to think we're fairly clever when we're helping Nancy with one of her mysteries. But when it comes right down to it, she's the one who does most of the heavy lifting, so to speak. Though I'd never really thought about it in so many words, George, Ned, and I pretty much take on the role of her sidekicks whenever strange things are afoot. It's a little strange to think of yourself as someone else's sidekick, but I can't think of a better way to describe it.

"I agree, Bess," Ned said. "So let's go over what we

have so far." He started ticking off things on his fingers, clearly slipping into young-reporter mode. "We know nobody's seen her since breakfast—at least no one we've found so far. We know she didn't take her cell phone."

"But she did take her car," George put in. "It wasn't at her house when we were there."

I glanced at her, impressed. I hadn't even thought to look for Nancy's car. I scanned my mind for something to contribute. "Don't forget that weird note on her calendar for tomorrow afternoon. That's the only thing we found that might have something to do with the museum mystery, right? We should try to figure out what it means in case she hasn't turned up by tomorrow."

As I said it, I gulped. Could Nancy still be missing tomorrow? It just seemed too strange and unpleasant to contemplate.

"What did the note say again?" George asked. "Something like RHC, MNY, right?"

"I forget the first part, but the second part was MHY HLL, I think." Suddenly I gasped as the answer popped into my head, bright as day—what Nancy would probably call a hunch, I suppose. "I've got it! That has to be short for Mahoney Hall, over at the university!"

Ned smacked himself on the forehead with the

flat of his hand. "Duh!" he exclaimed. "Of course it is. Why didn't we think of that before?"

George looked excited. "Cool. We can go there tomorrow at three o'clock and see what happens. Maybe that will tell us something!"

I knew how she felt. Finally we seemed to be getting somewhere. But we barely had a moment to enjoy what felt like our first serious breakthrough in the Case of the Missing Friend before I felt George stiffen beside me. Glancing over, I saw that she was glaring off into the crowd.

I knew that glare. Sure enough, when I followed her gaze, I saw Deirdre Shannon slouching toward us, a cute green sundress hanging off her slim shoulders and a handsome college-age guy trailing along behind her like a dog at her heel. And I don't mean a dog like Rufus, either. I'm talking about the other kind—the type of dog that would throw itself off a cliff if it thought that would earn it a pat or two. Deirdre does seem to attract that type somehow.

"Hello, boys and girls," she greeted us in her most supercilious tone. "Especially *boys,*" she purred, sidling a little closer to Ned. "So where's that red-headed ball and chain of yours tonight, Ned? Don't tell me she allowed you out to the festival alone?"

I should probably explain here that Deirdre has always had a thing for Ned, which is painfully obvious whenever she catches sight of him. It's kind of sad, really, especially since it's a lost cause—she has no chance at all with him. Luckily, her latest beau didn't seem to notice or care that she was flirting her little head off.

George definitely noticed though. She was gritting her teeth so hard it sounded like she was chewing on sandpaper.

Shooting her a cautionary glance—we didn't have time for an unpleasant scene—I forced a friendly smile. "Actually, Deirdre, it's funny you should mention Nancy," I said. "We were just looking for her. She—she's been missing in action all day, and we're getting a little worried."

George gaped at me in disbelief. "Why're you telling *her*?" she said, barely even attempting to keep her voice low. "It's not like she ever knows anything useful anyway."

That wasn't entirely true. As obnoxious as she can be, Deirdre has helped out more than once in the past when Nancy was on a case. Mostly by accident, true—but I figured we couldn't afford to pass up any possible help.

"Wait." A little smile was playing around the corners of Deirdre's perfectly crimson-lined lips. "Let me get this straight. Miss Nancy Drew, famous detective"—she drew the words out sarcastically, making them sound suspiciously like an insult—"has gone *missing*? Are you serious?"

Ned sighed. "That's right, Deirdre," he said patiently. "You haven't seen her today by any chance, have you?"

"Oh, dear," she cooed, giving Ned a pat on the arm. "I'm so sorry, Ned, but I haven't seen her in days. I'm sure you must be all distraught though. Perhaps I can keep an eye out for her from my float in the parade on Monday." She glanced around at George and me, looking even more pleased with herself than usual. "Oh, you *did* hear I've been elected Miss Rackham Industries, didn't you?"

"Really?" I said as politely as I could. "That's nice, Deirdre." I vaguely recalled reading something in the paper about a fancy new float being sponsored by Rackham Industries, the computer company that is the city's largest employer.

"Yes, it's quite an honor." Deirdre took the arm of her beau, who had been standing nearby, patient and slack-jawed, during the entire conversation. "Biff here is supposed to be my escort—his father is a very important man at Rackham Industries, you know. He plays golf with Daddy every weekend. Anyway, the float should really be something. A team of designers spent, like, ten thousand dollars to create it— they're still gluing on the exotic peacock feathers right now, I think. Oh! And then there's the crown I'll be wearing. That was specially commissioned too. They've even hired two trained guard dogs to protect it while it's at the Rackham Industries office this week. It's got over a hundred diamonds, and the gold to make the front part came directly from South Africa, and . . ."

She continued to brag about her crown, the float, and various other things for a little while. Finally she slowed down. I guess she got bored with us.

"Well, I can't stand around here chatting all night," she said abruptly. "Tell Nancy's kidnappers or whatever to let her out for the parade on Monday, okay? She won't want to miss seeing me in my moment of glory." With one last smirk she grabbed Biff's hand and dragged him off down the street.

"What a twit," George muttered as we hurried away in the opposite direction. "Miss Rackham Industries, indeed. What kind of bogus title is that, anyway? Miss Nerve-Racking Idiot is more like it!"

"Okay, where were we?" Ned said, clearly ready to forget about the whole scene and move on.

But George was still absorbed with Deirdre. "And did you hear her say she was 'elected' to the title? Yeah, right." She snorted. "It's obvious the only reason she was chosen was because of her father's stupid law firm—"

42

"George!" I said sharply. "Focus!"

But Ned suddenly stared at George thoughtfully. "Wait," he said. "Why is that ringing a bell?"

"Why is what ringing a bell?" George asked blankly.

I sighed. Why did I have the feeling we were turning into the Three Stooges of amateur sleuthing? It was probably just as well Nancy wasn't there to see us. . . .

"What you just said," Ned told George. "About Deirdre's dad's law firm—didn't we just see something about that?"

Finally I realized what he was driving at. "Sure," I said. "But it didn't have anything to do with Deirdre or the parade. It was one of the headlines on that news page, remember? His law firm is sponsoring the chess thingy at the museum."

"Oh, right!" George's puzzled expression cleared. "The traveling exhibit. What about it?"

Ned shrugged. "Just seems like a coincidence," he said. "Do you think it means anything, or am I just grasping at straws here?"

"Well, Nancy would probably say there aren't too many true coincidences," I pointed out diplomatically. "She's always looking for connections and stuff during her investigations, you know? So if she was here—"

George groaned. "Don't say it!"

"She'd probably want to find Deirdre again and talk to her some more, just in case it means something," I finished, with an apologetic shrug in George's direction.

"You're probably right." Ned didn't seem thrilled at the idea of spending more time with his not-so-secret admirer. But he squared his shoulders bravely. "Okay, let's go find her. She couldn't have gotten far. . . ."

We spent the next half hour searching fruitlessly through the crowd. Normally Deirdre is hard to miss at any gathering—she tends to try to make herself the center of attention whenever possible. But this time she seemed to have disappeared as completely as Nancy herself.

Finally, as the booths started closing up and the decorative strands of red-white-and-blue lights draped over the storefronts started winking off, we had to admit defeat. "Guess she went home," George said, stifling a yawn.

"I think we're going to have to do the same," I added reluctantly. "The crowd's really thinning out; we won't be able to find out much more here tonight."

We didn't say much to one another as we walked back to the car and rode toward home. "Let's be in touch first thing in the morning," Ned suggested as

George pulled up beside his car, which was still parked in front of the Drews' house. "That way, if she hasn't turned up by then . . ."

There was no need for him to finish the sentence. We all shuddered in unison. Then we headed home to our separate beds feeling disappointed, disgruntled, and inept.

"Everything will look better in the morning," I murmured to myself as I climbed into bed and, thankfully, fell almost immediately to sleep.

5

A New Lead

George

Sometime around the crack of dawn the next day, I became aware of an extremely irritating ringing sound filling my head. At first it was all mixed up with the scary new computer virus I was dreaming about, but eventually I swam upward through the dark fog of blissful sleep and realized the sound was all too real.

"Go 'way," I mumbled as I cracked open one eye and saw my little brother, Scott, hovering over my bed wearing his dorky Spider-Man pajamas. Sometimes I wonder if that kid is twelve years old or two.

"Get up, Georgia," Scott said way too loudly. "Phone's for you. Don't your friends know how to tell time?"

I opened my other eye, for one bleary moment

feeling annoyed and wondering if Nancy had gotten so excited about some new mystery or other that she'd forgotten some of us actually liked to sleep past five A.M. That sounded just like—

"Nancy!" I blurted out. Suddenly I sat bolt upright, wide awake, as the events of the previous day came flooding back over me. "Give me that phone," I demanded, snatching it out of Scott's hand. "Hello? Nancy, is that you?"

"Sorry," Ned's voice replied. "Just me. She—she hasn't turned up yet."

My heart sank like a stone. Maybe Miss Look-on-the-Bright-Side Bess was rubbing off on me, but I realized I'd really, really been hoping that I'd wake up and find that Nancy had returned overnight. I'd even imagined her laughing sheepishly as she explained away her temporary disappearance with some goofy Nancy-type explanation, like she'd managed to get stranded fifty miles outside of town in some deserted area and had to walk back. Nancy's probably the only person in the world who can run out of gas in an electric-hybrid car. I don't know how she does it. Then again, there's Bess's theory, which is that Nancy never actually runs out of gas at all, but uses that as a cover story so we won't find out she's accidentally locked her keys in the car for the ten millionth time. Someday, someone needs to invent some kind of device to solve *that* little problem. . . .

Realizing that my still-half-asleep mind was wandering well off track, I did my best to focus on what Ned was saying, which was something about going to work. "Um what?" I asked, stifling a yawn. "Sorry, didn't catch that last part."

"I said, I'm wondering if I should call the *Bugle* and say I can't make it in today. I'd have already done that, but there's just a skeleton crew in the office all weekend, starting Friday, because of the holiday, and I'm supposed to cover Monday's parade, and—"

"Oh," I said, finally catching on to what he was talking about so anxiously. Ned works part-time at the *Bugle*—he's sort of a combo junior-reporter/gofer/fact-checker. Of course, being the boss's son means he probably doesn't have to do as much of the gofering as the junior-reportering. Then again, being Mr. Eagle Scout, he probably volunteers for the gofering.

Oops. More mind wandering.

"Don't sweat it," I told Ned, switching the phone to my other ear as I swung my legs over the edge of the bed and stood up. "Bess and I are on the case. We'll keep you posted if we figure out anything important."

Ned paused for so long that I started to think we'd lost the connection. "Well . . . okay," he said at last. "I guess there's not a whole lot I could do out there.

And maybe I'll hear something useful at the office. At the very least, I can look into this whole museum angle a little more while I'm there."

"That's the spirit." I yawned again. "Maybe Bess and I can come pick you up when you get off. If Nancy hasn't turned up by then, that is."

"Right." Ned's voice cracked a little, revealing his anxiety. "See you then."

I'd barely hung up the phone when it rang again. "What, did River Heights suddenly shift to a different time zone when I wasn't looking?" I muttered, punching the Talk button. "Hello?"

"It's me," Bess's voice said, sounding annoyingly chipper for that hour of the morning. "Did you talk to Ned?"

"Would I sound this awake if I hadn't?" I countered.

Bess giggled. "Well, pour some caffeine down your throat and get ready," she warned. "I'll be over there in, like, ten minutes."

I was only on my second cup of coffee—no milk, four tablespoons of sugar—when Bess burst in through the kitchen door. It's really kind of eerie how, even at six A.M., she can manage to look like she just stepped out of the fashion pages. She was wearing pink tennis shoes that perfectly matched her pink gingham blouse, her blond hair was pulled back in a perky ponytail, and her face managed to look fresh and dewy-perfect with no obvious evidence of makeup, though I suspected she'd applied some. Next to her I probably looked like the Creature from the Black Lagoon in my stained terrycloth bathrobe and faded red flip-flops, my eyes half closed, pillow creases on one cheek, and my hair still spiked up from sleep.

"Where's the fashion show?" I asked grumpily.

She ignored me, bustling over to help herself to a cup of coffee. Lots of milk, half a tablespoon of sugar. "Listen, I've been thinking," she said briskly as she sat down across from me. "If we're going to find Nancy today, we're going to have to get organized."

I squinted at her suspiciously, recognizing her chipper demeanor. That's how Bess sometimes gets when in a real crisis. Her naturally sunny personality won't allow her to get grumpy and depressed like a regular person, so she hides her anxiety beneath a veneer of energetic, efficient chirpiness. It was a sure sign to me that she was worried, really worried.

And no wonder. Nancy had been missing for almost twenty-four hours now. What had seemed yesterday like a mildly worrisome puzzler was definitely starting to seem now like a full-blown crisis. People like Nancy Drew don't just disappear without a reason, and all of the possible reasons I could come up with weren't good news.

"You're right," I told Bess, gulping down another swig of my coffee in the hopes that it would clear my head and make it easier to think about what to do. In case you haven't figured it out by now, I'm not exactly a morning person. "Should we type up some notes on the computer?"

We moved ourselves, and our coffee, up to the large, cluttered desk in my bedroom. Shoving aside a few modems I was trying to repair in my spare time, I logged on to my desktop and opened a blank document.

"Okay," I said, my fingers poised over the keyboard. "What do we know so far?"

"We know Nancy is missing," Bess replied with a shrug. "And has been since yesterday. Nobody we've spoken to so far has seen her since she left her house at around nine o'clock yesterday morning."

I nodded, typing rapidly. "Right. We also know she was on to some kind of mystery-type thing at the museum. . . ."

It took a depressingly short time to type in everything we knew so far. The e-mail about the museum mystery. The missed dates. The notations on her calendar.

"And then there are the things that probably don't mean anything," Bess added, reading over what I'd written. "Like that one e-mail from the unknown sender. And the stuff about Deirdre's dad's firm."

I groaned. "Oh, yeah," I muttered, recalling our irritating conversation—or should that be *monologue*?—with Deirdre. "Well, if we're going to talk to her again, I say we should just get it over with."

I grabbed the cell phone off my bedside table and punched in Deirdre's name. My phone has this cool feature that automatically looks up any number from the River Heights phone book, which I'd downloaded from my computer. The number dialed itself almost immediately. One ring, then two, three, four . . .

"Wait, George. Don't you think—"

Before Bess could finish her sentence, someone finally picked up on the other end. "What?"

Deirdre's phone had just been answered by a large, cranky frog. But I thought I detected a familiar snooty tone beneath the croakiness. "Uh—Deirdre?" I said.

"Who is this?" The frogginess was fading, replaced by Deirdre's distinctive snarl. "Who's there? If this is the jerk who's been crank calling me, I'd better warn you, my father is a lawyer and he's going to sue your—"

"Deirdre! No, wait. It's me." I cleared my throat, belatedly realizing it was still only a few minutes after six in the morning. On a Saturday. "Uh, it's George Fayne."

"What?" Instead of reassuring her, my identity seemed to make her crankier than ever. "What do *you* want? Do you know what time it is?"

I rolled my eyes as Bess grinned. It wasn't like I was any more thrilled to be talking to Deirdre than she was to hear from me. "Er, whatever, sorry about that," I said. "But listen, this is important, okay? Nancy still hasn't turned up yet, and we just wanted to ask you a little more about—"

She didn't even let me finish. "You can ask me stuff at a more reasonable hour," she snapped. There was a click, and the connection went dead.

I sighed and hung up. "Oops," I said weakly as Bess smirked. "Maybe we can try her again later."

We had barely returned to discussing our pathetic little list of clues when Mr. Drew called. He sounded weary and haggard even over the phone, and I wondered if he'd slept.

"Sorry for calling so early," he said. "I hope I didn't wake you."

"It's okay. We're up," I replied. "Bess is here now, and we're trying to figure out what to do next."

"Good, good." He sounded distracted. "Listen, I just wanted to remind you kids to keep an eye out for Nancy's car, too. It still hasn't turned up either. I told the police it's gone, of course, but I thought if you all were out and about today—"

"Gotcha," I replied. "Will do."

After I hung up, I told Bess what Nancy's father had said. "That's a good point," she commented. "Nancy's car is pretty distinctive; there still aren't too many of those hybrids in River Heights. So maybe we should start asking people about that."

"Hey, I know who we can ask first," I said, picking up the phone again. "Charlie Adams. He knows that car as well as anyone—if it's around town today, he'll spot it."

Charles Adams is a few years older than my friends and I and works for a local garage. He's the one who usually comes to the rescue when Nancy's stranded. Bess thinks he's a little sweet on Nancy—he hardly ever charges her for his services, and gets a little tongue-tied whenever she's around. I figured that could only help our cause.

Sure enough, Charlie sounded concerned when he heard that Nancy was missing. "But I can solve the mystery of her missing car right now," he said, speaking rapidly. "It's right here in the shop. Busted tire."

"Oh!" I was surprised. "Er, when did that happen?"

"Yesterday around nine thirty or ten A.M.," Charlie replied. "When Nancy called, I went to pick up the car and bring it in right away. Brought it straight into the shop."

"Do you know where Nancy went after that?" I

pressed the phone tightly to my ear, not wanting to miss a word. If what Charlie was saying was accurate, he was the last one to see Nancy before her disappearance. I'm not real big on Nancy-style hunches, but I wondered if this could be the break we were waiting for.

"Sure enough," Charlie replied to my question. "After we got the car here, she asked me to drop her off at Anvil Park. I offered to wait till she was done with whatever she had to do, but she said she could get herself home from there."

I thanked him and hung up, then glanced at Bess. She was staring at me anxiously.

"Well?" she asked.

I stood up and stretched. "Let me just throw on some clothes," I said. "We're going to Anvil Park."

Anvil Park is a small but attractive public green space near the university. Its name comes from the enormous anvil sculpture that dominates its central fountain. Anvils are big in River Heights, since that was the industry on which the city was founded back in the day. In addition to the fountain, the park contains flower gardens, stately trees, and several flat, lush lawns where townspeople and college students alike often come to picnic or play Frisbee.

"Okay," Bess said as I pulled to the curb at the

edge of the park. "So what are we looking for here?"

I shrugged. To be honest, I wasn't sure. "Anything weird or suspicious, I guess," I said. "We can talk to people, see if anyone was here yesterday and saw Nancy. . . ."

The plan sounded a little lame, even to me. But this still felt like the only real lead we'd had so far. Well, except for that calendar notation, and there were still hours to go before we could check into that.

It was the beginning of another beautiful midwestern midsummer day, and there were a bunch of people in the park even at that early hour running and playing with their dogs. Bess and I wandered around for a while, discussing the case and stopping to talk to people now and then. Once again, nobody we spoke with had any idea where Nancy might be.

Bess let out a sigh. "You know, this is starting to feel kind of random." She brushed away a stray strand of blond hair and glanced around the park with a troubled expression in her blue eyes. "I'm afraid we might just be wasting time. If Nancy was here . . ."

I frowned. "If Nancy was here, we wouldn't be looking for her," I said sharply. "But she's not, so we have to do whatever we . . . Hey! There's Mr. Geffington. He's a major busybody—let's go talk to him."

I'd just spotted the portly, gray-haired manager of the First Bank of River Heights. Bradley Geffington is a fussy man with a tendency to spend way too much time worrying about what all his neighbors are doing.

As we hurried toward him across a small, sunny lawn, I let Bess take the lead. She has a magic touch with people, especially men. Even more especially men prone to flattery, like Mr. Geffington.

"Oh, my," Geffington said when he heard what we were doing there. "Young Nancy Drew missing? That's quite— Look out!"

I stared at him in surprise as his eyes suddenly went round and wide with alarm. He jabbed one pudgy finger urgently at something behind me.

Perplexed, I quickly glanced over my shoulder, prepared to dodge a tennis ball or dog bone. But I wasn't at all prepared for what I saw.

A huge, snarling beast was leaping straight toward me!

6

Checkmates

Bess

I screamed as I turned and saw a monster-size, muscular black dog rushing at George. My cousin's face went white, and she seemed to be frozen in place, staring helplessly into the creature's slavering jaws.

"Hans!" a sharp voice barked out from somewhere nearby, aggressive and firm. "Halt! Down!"

Instantly the dog dropped in place, crouching over its own paws just a few feet in front of George. Turning to search out the sound of the voice, I saw a middle-aged woman hurrying toward us. She had short-cropped reddish brown hair and a rather stocky build that wasn't particularly flattered by the drab olive-colored sweatpants and the gray T-shirt she was wearing. She was carrying a leather-and-chain leash in one hand.

As she reached us, the dog glanced up at her with a whimper, its stubby tail wagging uncertainly. The woman leaned over to pat the dog. "Good boy, Hans," she cooed. Then she straightened up and glared at us. "What are you people doing here?" she snapped. "Don't you realize you could have been hurt if Hans had attacked? Everybody knows I'm here at this time of day!"

I goggled at her, amazed at her rudeness. "Excuse me?" I exclaimed. "This is a public park, and we—"

She almost immediately bowled over my words with more of her own. "I'm here every day of the week at seven A.M. on the dot," she ranted, sounding quite proud of her self-proclaimed punctuality. "It's the only convenient place around here with the space I need, and consistency is vital to my work. These animals are very valuable and finely tuned, and need plenty of exercise. And that means every day of the week. Dog training is no holiday, you know."

George had finally recovered her voice after her close call. "Are you insane?" she demanded, pointing a slightly shaking finger at Hans. "That thing could've killed me!"

"Miss Fayne is quite right," Mr. Geffington spoke up firmly, casting a cautious eye at the dog, which hadn't moved anything but its watchful eyes since dropping to the ground. "That beast seems rather—er—excitable."

The woman blinked at the bank manager, seeming to see him for the first time. "Oh, hello," she said, her voice suddenly changing from an angry growl to a rough purr. "Aren't you Mr. Bradley Geffington?"

"Why yes, yes I am." Mr. Geffington puffed out his chest, looking pleased to be recognized. "And you are? . . ."

"Marge Kurz." The woman stuck out her hand to shake. At her feet Hans peered up at Geffington suspiciously.

"Er, good morning, Ms. Kurz." Mr. Geffington took the woman's hand gingerly, carefully keeping his feet well away from the prone dog. "Now, this animal of yours is very impressive, but it seems rather dangerous to leave him loose to leap about like that."

"Oh, but it's not as simple as that," Ms. Kurz said, her voice now silky smooth, as if she'd given this reply many times before. "My dogs aren't pets by any means—they're hair-trigger protection devices. I train them for specialty clients in need of extra security—perhaps like your bank, Mr. Geffington?" She smiled at him. "Hans here is just a youngster—imported him from Germany just a couple of months ago." She bent and ruffled the dog's ears fondly. "We're still working on his basic commands. Luckily

60

he's learning fast." She shot George a slightly sour look before returning her full attention to Mr. Geffington. "When he progresses a bit more in his training, I'll change the ordinary command words to secret commands that only the client who hires or buys him will be told. That way, a potential thief can't control the dog by using regular commands." She paused and smiled again at the bank manager. "Oh, and I require only two-thirds of my fee paid up front if you should happen to be interested."

"Fascinating." Despite his polite comment, Mr. Geffington looked slightly bored. I caught him sneaking a peek at his gold-plated watch.

Ms. Kurz moved a little closer, muttering something about giving Mr. Geffington her card. I couldn't help finding the dog trainer's manner a little grating, but now that the moment of terror had passed, I was eager to smooth things over. If she was at the park every morning, maybe she had seen Nancy the day before.

"Are you new in town, Ms. Kurz?" I asked politely, figuring there was nothing like a little small talk to prepare her for my questions. "Because if you're looking for new clients, I might know a dog that could use a little discipline." I winked at George, thinking of Mr. Pembleton's dog, Rufus, from the day before. "Like how to heel for his owner, instead of dragging him all over town . . ."

Ms. Kurz was already wrinkling her nose with dis-taste. "I'm sorry, young lady, but I don't do that," she told me, her voice dripping with condescension. "As I said, I specialize in highly trained protection dogs for a select clientele. I don't do pet classes." She put extra emphasis on the word *pet,* making it sound like some kind of disgusting disease or something.

"Well, goody for you," George said under her breath, though I'm not sure Ms. Kurz heard her. She was too busy chattering at Mr. Geffington, following him as he edged away toward the park entrance.

"Come, Hans," she said.

I glanced nervously at Hans, who had lifted his head to watch his mistress depart. He whined anx-iously, then carefully climbed to his feet and padded after her without so much as a glance at me or my cousin.

After a brief debate, George and I decided not to bother following to question her. "If she just moved here, she probably doesn't even know Nancy," George pointed out. "Besides, she strikes me as the type who doesn't notice other people unless they happen to be in her way or something. Or caught in her dog's teeth."

That seemed a little harsh, but I had to admit she might be right. I couldn't really blame George for wanting to keep some distance between herself and Hans. Not that I'd ever say so, of course. George would never admit to being scared, and would probably insist on rushing over to wrestle the dog if I even hinted at it. But he looked pretty fierce.

"So what do we do now?" I asked instead.

"I guess it's time to go over our notes again." I could tell George had no more idea how to proceed than I did, but didn't want to admit that, either. In that case, I knew how she felt.

Realizing we were both hungry—it's funny how a near-death experience whets the appetite—we wandered over to the College Diner and ordered a late breakfast. That consisted of pancakes and bacon for George and an egg-white omelet for me. As usual, I couldn't resist a tiny flash of envy as I saw her tucking into her food. All our lives George has had the ability to eat like a longshoreman but still stay thin as a rail. I'm not the type to follow diet fads or deny myself the foods I really love, but I still have to watch what I eat pretty carefully to avoid blowing up like a puffer fish.

I shooed away such thoughts quickly, feeling terribly shallow for even having them at a time like this. "All right," I said briskly. "Let's go over what we've done so far. We've talked to at least two dozen people, and nobody has seen Nancy since Charlie dropped her off at the park yesterday morning. We know she can't have gone far on her own without her car—"

"And we still don't know what this whole mystery museum stuff might be about," George added, popping a piece of bacon into her mouth.

I'd just cut a small piece of omelet and lifted it to my mouth, but I set it down without eating it. Even after all we'd done so far, we still had no idea what had happened to our friend. For all we knew she could be trapped somewhere, hurt or scared or . . .

"She's missing," I said, fear taking hold of my stomach and squeezing any appetite right out of it. "She's really missing, George."

As soon as the words left my mouth, I prepared myself for a "duh" kind of reaction from George. Instead she stared somberly at me across the table. "Yeah," she said. "I know."

George and I were waiting at the curb in her car when Ned emerged from the *Bugle* building that afternoon at 2:45, looking as handsome as ever in a pair of khakis and a striped polo. He was supposed to work until 3:00 that day, but we'd called to see if he could get out a little early so we could all go over to Mahoney Hall to follow up on that calendar clue.

Ned hurried across the sidewalk and slid into the backseat. "Anything to report?" he asked hopefully.

George and I exchanged a glance. After leaving the

diner, we'd spent the next several hours wandering around town, trying to figure out what to do and questioning anyone we came across. We'd even tried to call Deirdre again, but nobody had answered at her house, and we didn't have her cell phone number.

"Sorry," George told Ned. "Our investigation has pretty much been a bust so far." George did quickly fill Ned in on what she learned from Charlie Adams, but the information wasn't all that helpful or inspiring.

"But don't worry," I added quickly as Ned's face fell. "This three o'clock thing is our big clue, right? So maybe this will be the big breakthrough we're waiting for!"

I don't know exactly what I was expecting when we reached Mahoney Hall—maybe a big dramatic ransom note scrawled on the wall explaining exactly what had happened to our friend, or better yet, Nancy herself locked up in a room just waiting for us to come rescue her. Instead the only thing we found going on in the entire building was a meeting of the River Heights Chess Society.

"Well, that fits with the clue, I guess," George said blankly. "RHCSoc, remember?"

Ned nodded, looking equally perplexed as he stared through the small glass window in the door leading into the meeting room. "Sounds like this is it, all right," he agreed. "But why would she make a note about this meeting? Nancy's not a member of the chess club. Do you think this could have something to do with that chess exhibit at the museum? Could that be the connection here?"

Neither George nor I had an answer for that. "As long as we're here, we might as well go in and ask around," I suggested. "Maybe someone will be able to tell us something useful."

We pushed open the door and walked in, apologizing for the interruption. The chess club membership was fairly small—there were only about a dozen people in all. Among those present were Evaline Waters and Marcus Pembleton, who were sitting together near the front of the room. Just behind them I spotted an attractive brunette in her late twenties. She waved when she saw us, making the silver bracelets on her arm jingle.

"Hi, Simone," I greeted her. "I didn't know you were a chess fan."

Simone Valinkofsky had moved to River Heights from France just a short while before. She lived a few blocks from Nancy and had once required her help to retrieve a valuable Fabergé egg that was also a cherished family heirloom. Since then, Simone had thrown herself wholeheartedly into her new community, volunteering for some of the same charities as Nancy, along with various local political causes.

"Yes, I love the game," Simone replied in her soft accent. "I'm afraid I'm not very good though."

"Nonsense!" Marcus Pembleton had overheard her. He beamed at her with delight. "Young Miss V is a very clever player, quite the stylist, really. Plus, it doesn't hurt that any man who looks into her lovely eyes tends to forget the difference between a bishop and a pawn." He winked broadly as Simone blushed and the others in the room chuckled.

"Enough, Marcus," Ms. Waters scolded him playfully. "You don't want to embarrass dear Simone. She may not come back, and then the club will be stuck with just a lot of old coots like you and me."

Everyone smiled again. Well, everyone except George. I could practically feel her quivering with impatience beside me.

"Listen," she said abruptly. "We don't want to take up too much of your time. But we really need to know if any of you have seen or spoken to our friend Nancy Drew in the past day or so."

Simone raised an eyebrow. "Oh! It's funny you should mention Nancy. We were just wondering if she might show up here today—she'd asked me for information on our next meeting when I saw her last week."

"That's not too likely, I'm afraid," Ned said grimly. "Nancy seems to be missing. No one has seen hide nor hair of her since early yesterday morning."

The room erupted in gasps and exclamations of dismay. I glanced around quickly. I couldn't let go of the idea that this meeting was significant somehow. If not, why would Nancy have noted it so carefully? As far as I knew, she had no particular interest in chess, though she and her father played occasionally. Could someone here know something about her disappearance? Scanning the familiar faces—Ms. Waters, Mr. Pembleton, Simone, popular university professor Clay Simmons, local fire chief Cody Cloud—it didn't seem too likely.

I guess my friends were thinking the same thing. Ned sounded subdued and slightly perfunctory as he asked the group a few questions about their meetings.

"This particular meeting is an extra one this week," Ms. Waters said in response to Ned's query about whether they always met at the same time. "You may have noticed we don't have any chess sets with us today."

She waved one slender hand around the room. I realized I hadn't noticed, which made me feel slightly sheepish. It was just the type of detail Nancy would have noted immediately upon entering.

"You see," Ms. Waters continued, "we wanted to get together today before all the weekend hullabaloo starts, so we can plan the little field trip we intend to take next week. I'm sure you've heard about the chess exhibit opening next week at the museum?"

The three of us murmured our assent. Once again I glanced sharply around the room, wondering if anyone there would react to the mention of the museum. That would be a good clue.

But the faces that gazed back at me were clouded only with concern and curiosity. After a few more questions, we thanked the club members and took our leave.

"Well, that told us a big fat lot of nothing," George said gloomily as we stepped out of the building and headed down the sidewalk toward her car. "We're totally pathetic, do you realize that? Nancy's been missing for, like, a day and a half now, and we've figured out exactly zippo about where she might be or what could have happened to her. Some detectives we are!"

She kicked at the ground, her face set into an angry scowl. Ned didn't look much happier.

"Okay, so maybe we're not looking like supersleuths right now," I said. "But we can't give up! Nancy never gives up when one of her leads or theories doesn't pan out, right? Besides, there's one loose end we still need to investigate. . . ." I hesitated and glanced at George, expecting her to protest or at least roll her eyes.

Instead she nodded firmly. "Good point," she said. "It's time to track down Deirdre and find out if she knows anything useful for once."

7

New Directions

George

Bess, Ned, and I might not be the brightest bunch of detectives in the world without Nancy around to guide us, but at least we managed to solve one mystery that day. It took us no time at all to track down Deirdre at her parents' country club. Luckily a school friend of Ned's was working at the reception desk at the club and let us in, even though none of us were members.

We found Deirdre lounging in one of the teak steamer chairs by the pool. A glass of iced tea sat on a matching teak table at her elbow, and a fashion magazine lay open across her stomach. Her pale skin glistened with lotion, and wraparound sunglasses hid her eyes.

"Cute bathing suit," Bess murmured under her breath as we approached.

I rolled my eyes. The red and gold bikini Deirdre was wearing didn't look like anything special to me, though judging by the impressed look on Bess's face, it was probably some kind of designer original or something.

Stopping beside her chair, I waited for her to acknowledge our presence. When she didn't, I cleared my throat loudly.

Deirdre twitched and flipped up her dark glasses. "Huh?" she grunted, squinting at me. "Oh. Fayne. What are you doing here?" Suddenly spotting Ned standing behind me, she smiled. "Oh! Hi, Ned. Did your parents finally join the club?"

"Not exactly." Ned stepped forward. "We were just looking for you."

"Well, here I am." Deirdre sat up, resting her weight on one arm and smiling up at him silkily. "So what can I do for you?"

Even though it was abundantly clear that she wasn't talking to me, I spoke up. "We have some questions for you."

In case I'd had any doubts about the depth of Deirdre's self-absorption—which I hadn't—she seemed to have no recollection of Nancy's disappearance until I mentioned it again.

"Oh, right," she said with a shrug. "She still hasn't turned up yet, huh? Bummer."

"Yes," Ned replied calmly. I don't know how he did it; I felt like punching Deirdre right in her snooty face. "So we're just trying to gather as much information as possible, to try to figure out where she might have gone."

Deirdre rolled her eyes. "Are you sure it's a good time to be playing little Nancy-type detective games?" she said lazily. "I mean, if she's really missing, maybe you should leave things to the police."

It was probably the closest she'd ever come to insulting Ned. Well, except for her usual insults about his taste in girlfriends, of course.

"Look, are you going to answer our questions or not?" I was rapidly running out of patience with her.

Ned and Bess both shot me warning glances. "We were just remembering the stuff you were saying last night about the parade," Bess put in. "You know—the big, fancy float you'll be riding?"

Deirdre suddenly looked much more interested in the conversation. "Wait until you see it," she said smugly. "It's going to blow away the competition in the contest."

"Contest?" I repeated. "What contest?"

Ned glanced at me. "Didn't you hear?" he asked. "The Mahoney Foundation is sponsoring a parade competition this year. There will be awards for stuff like most creative float, best band, most city spirit—"

"And best float," Deirdre added. "That would be mine. They might as well hand over the prize right now, because no one will be able to beat us."

I couldn't let that ridiculous assertion go by unchallenged. "Don't be too sure about that," I snapped. "If it's anything like past years, there are going to be an awful lot of cool floats. The library does a great one every year, and the high school's float is usually pretty good, and then there was that one last year that all the local antiques shops put together. . . ."

Deirdre snorted. "Amateur hour," she drawled, settling back on her chair. "None of those groups have Rackham money behind them, do they?"

That seemed to settle the question in her tiny mind, and she quickly moved on to bragging about her crown again. Noticing that a couple of club employees were shooting us suspicious looks, my friends and I took the earliest possible opportunity to escape.

Outside in the club's oak-shaded parking lot, we huddled by my car and talked over what we'd just learned. Which wasn't much.

"Okay, that was kind of a waste of time," Bess admitted, glancing over her shoulder at the club.

"Maybe not." Ned scratched his chin thoughtfully. "What about that float contest? Could there be something in that maybe?"

We all stared at one another for a moment. I tried

to imagine what possible connection the parade contest could have with Nancy's disappearance, but came up empty.

"Is the museum sponsoring a float for the parade?" Bess asked uncertainly. "If so, maybe that has something to do with Nancy's e-mail. Maybe someone is trying to fix the contest. Or sabotage the museum's float. Or something."

"I'm not sure," Ned said. "I know the university is doing a float. But I don't know if the museum is part of that, or if they're doing something separately."

I could tell we were grasping at straws, hunting for any possible connection that might give us a lead to follow. "This is getting ridiculous," I said with frustration. "We still don't have any real suspects. Or any good clues. Or any likely motives."

"Motives," Ned said. "Hmm . . ."

"What?" I stared at him.

He shrugged. "Are we missing the point here?" he wondered. "I mean, we keep trying to fit Nancy's disappearance in with that museum mystery somehow. But what if that's just a red herring? Unfortunately there are plenty of people out there who probably don't think too kindly of Nancy—namely, all the tons of criminals she's helped put away over the years. What if one of them decided it's time for a little revenge?"

Bess gasped. "You really think that's possible?" she exclaimed. "That Nancy could have been kidnapped? But all those people deserved to go to jail—surely they wouldn't really try to get back at Nancy that way. Would they?"

She sounded completely shocked at the very idea. No surprise there. Bess always wants to think the best of people. She'd probably make excuses for a pickpocket as he was slipping her wallet out of her purse.

"I don't think we can rule anything out," Ned replied grimly.

I shivered as I realized just how right he was. "Maybe we should call Chief McGinnis and see if he's thought of the possibility that this could be a revenge thing," I said, already digging into my pocket for my cell phone. "I'll give him a call right now."

As it turned out, Chief McGinnis had thought of that possibility. It also turned out he wasn't thrilled to be interrupted to hear about it again while he was in the middle of a family barbecue.

"Is that all, Miss Fayne?" he asked, sounding rather grumpy. "Because the burgers are about to be overdone, so . . ."

"Sorry, Chief. Enjoy your burgers." I hung up, feeling sheepish. But that feeling was soon overtaken by irritation. "What's his problem, anyway?" I grumbled as I tucked my phone away. "I mean,

Nancy has been missing for way more than twenty-four hours now! Why are we the only ones who seem to be worried about her?"

"Don't forget Mr. Drew and Hannah," Bess reminded me quietly. "They're frantic too. Maybe we should call them, tell them what we're thinking."

"I've been thinking about that too, George," Mr. Drew said somberly when I reached him by phone and told him our disgruntled-criminal theory. "In fact, I've been working my contacts all day, trying to figure out who might have both motive and opportunity to do Nancy harm."

"Good plan," I said. "Maybe we'll do the same." When I hung up, I glanced at Ned. "Hey," I said. "Feel like going back to work for a while?"

He nodded. "Exactly what I was thinking."

We spent the next hour or two in front of a bank of computers at the *Bugle* offices. As Ned had mentioned, most of the staff was off for the holiday weekend. I'm not sure if that's why nobody bothered us or even asked what Bess and I were doing there, or if it had more to do with the fact that we were with the publisher's son.

Anyone who knows me will tell you there's not much I love more than messing around on the computer. But after staring fixedly at screen after screen full of news releases, news wire services, and other articles detailing local crime over the past few years, my eyes were starting to glaze over.

"Finding anything useful?" I asked the others, leaning back and rubbing my eyes so hard I saw sparks. "Because as far as I can tell, most of the perps Nancy busted are either still in jail, or live about ten billion miles from River Heights."

"Same here," Ned said. "I've found a few names we can check into, but mostly I'm hitting dead ends. I've been thinking about something else. What if the bad guy we're looking for isn't mad because of something Nancy did. What's if he's trying to get back at her father? He's put quite a few nasty types away himself, you know."

That thought hadn't occurred to me. "Oh, man," I said, staring at him. "If that's the case, there must be about half a million—"

"Hey, guys," Bess said at that moment, interrupting me. She was staring at her computer screen with a puzzled look on her face. "Why does this guy seem so weirdly familiar? Do you remember this case?"

I leaned over to take a look. The first thing I saw on the page she'd pulled up was an old photo of Nancy, probably taken somewhere around our freshman year of high school. Beside it was a picture of a scowling young man with a beaklike nose and heavy brows.

"Doesn't look familiar," I said, peering at the slightly grainy photo. "Who is he?"

"It's that guy who was running that phone scam, remember?" Bess said. "Nancy figured it out by pretending to let him sucker her in. . . . I sort of remember the case, but I don't know why his name keeps bugging me all of sudden. Zane Quinn?"

"It is kind of a funny name," Ned said with a shrug. "Maybe you just—"

I gasped, suddenly putting two and two together. "No, I know why!" I exclaimed. "Zane Quinn—ZQ." I jabbed a finger excitedly at the scowling photo. "This must be the guy who e-mailed Nancy this week! ZQ something-or-other, remember? I mean, how many people have those initials?"

Ned was still reading the article over Bess's shoulder. "I don't know," he said. "But I don't think he's our guy. According to this, he should still be in jail for another couple of years."

"Are you sure?" I suddenly went all deflated. For a second there, it had almost felt like we were getting somewhere.

"Well, we can check into it, I guess." Ned stifled a yawn. "Maybe you can do a search on his name or something. But we should probably call about some of the other names I found before it gets too late. You know—focus our attention for now on those we know are definitely back out on the street."

I had to admit that made sense. "Okay, give me the list," I said. "I'll start calling." I paused. "And I've been thinking about something too," I added. "If someone grabbed Nancy and is, like, holding her hostage or whatever, why hasn't there been a ransom note yet? Isn't that how kidnappers usually work?"

"Good question." From the way he said it, I guessed that Ned had already thought of that. And no wonder. It was just one of the many things about this case that didn't make much sense. "I don't know. I just hope she's . . ."

He let his voice trail off without finishing. I shuddered, not wanting to think about what he'd been about to say. "Okay," I said, grabbing for a nearby phone. "You guys keep surfing. I'll start calling."

By late that night we'd managed to rule out quite a few possibilities in terms of potential kidnappers. By calling various jails, police departments, and private homes, we'd figured out the whereabouts of most of the criminals and ex-cons on our list, and had determined that they hadn't been anywhere near River Heights in the past week. It felt almost like real detective work. There was just one problem—we were still no closer to knowing what had become of Nancy.

"All we know is these guys couldn't have snatched

her," I said, tossing down the list of names and phone numbers and rubbing my ear, which was numb from being pressed to the phone receiver.

"That's more than we knew a couple of hours ago," Bess pointed out. Despite her typically optimistic words, her voice sounded tired and worried.

"True." Ned stifled a yawn and glanced at the large clock on the office wall. "But it's almost midnight—we probably shouldn't make any more calls this late. Maybe we should call it a night, and start again bright and early in the morning."

I hated the thought that another day had passed and we still hadn't even come close to finding Nancy. Hated it a lot. But what could we do? Ned was right.

"Guess so," I said with a deep sigh. "Come on, I'll drive you guys home."

8

Free-Floating Anxiety

Bess

This is crazy," George burst out irritably. "It's like she just fell off the face of the earth!"

I set down the doughnut I'd just picked up, feeling tears gathering in my eyes. It was Sunday morning, and there had been no word from Nancy. George, Ned, and I were sitting in my kitchen drinking coffee and trying to choke down a little food before we headed out to continue our investigation.

Ned rubbed his eyes, which looked tired and bloodshot from lack of sleep. "Look, we just have to focus," he said wearily. "She's got to be somewhere. Let's review our notes again—we must be missing something."

George shrugged, then opened her laptop computer,

which she'd brought with her. "Okay," she said. "But we don't have much."

She quickly read through the things we'd noted over the past two days—the mysterious e-mail about the museum, the car story from Charlie Adams, the notes on Nancy's calendar, and the stuff we'd learned about Deirdre's float.

"You're right, that's not much." Ned sighed, drumming his fingers so hard on the tabletop that my coffee cup rattled. "This is so frustrating—it seems like we've followed all the leads we could think of. We researched the museum angle, you guys checked out that park where Charlie dropped her off, we even talked to Deirdre. What else can we do?"

"We can keep on talking to people around town," I suggested. "Nancy always says there's no such thing as an unsolvable mystery. Sometimes you just need to look harder for the clues, so I guess that's what we have to do. Someone must know something about her whereabouts; we just have to find that person."

"Good point." Ned nodded. "Maybe we should start being more organized about doing that. We could go around street by street, starting down there by the park, and ask people who work in the shops and other businesses nearby if they saw her that day. That way we might be able to figure out if Charlie really was the last one to see her, or if she went somewhere else after leaving the park."

"That sounds like a good idea, except for one thing," George said. "Most of the businesses downtown are closed today, even the ones that are normally open on Sundays."

I nodded and bit my lip, knowing she was right. The entire city would be distracted that day, either enjoying the festival or preparing frantically for tomorrow's big parade.

George stared at her laptop's small screen. "All our clues and leads just seem so random," she mused, more to herself than to us. "Like they're totally unrelated to one another. And maybe totally unrelated to Nancy."

"I know." I stirred my coffee as I gazed worriedly at my friends. "I don't know how Nancy does this all the time. It never seems this hard when she's around."

George shot me a quick glance, and an even quicker smile. "Sure it does," she said. "It's just that this confusing part never lasts that long, because being confused just makes Nancy even more determined to figure things out."

"You know, you're right." I cracked a smile too. "She never gives up on a case. That means we can't give up either—if Chief McGinnis ends up being the one to find her instead of us, she'll never let us live it down."

It was a pretty weak joke, but George chuckled.

"Deal," she said. "So let's stop complaining, figure out what to do next, and do it."

I glanced over at Ned and found him staring blankly into space. I wasn't sure if he'd even heard the last few minutes of our conversation. "You know, I just realized we never really talked about that other note on her calendar."

"What other note?" George pushed away her laptop and reached for a doughnut. "You mean the thing about the parade? I thought we decided she was just reminding herself to go watch."

"But the wording was a little strange," Ned pointed out. "It didn't really sound like something Nancy would write as a simple reminder note. Besides, who in River Heights could possibly forget about the July Fourth parade? Even Nancy isn't *that* absentminded."

He had a point. "What did it say again?" I asked.

George leaned toward her laptop. "Here it is, I wrote it down," she said. "That note said *'parade, watch then—comm. as cover?'*"

"Comm," I repeated. "That must be short for something. Community? Communists? Committee?"

"Your guess is as good as mine," Ned admitted, rubbing his chin. "But I just thought of something. What if it's a clue as to what the museum mystery is really about? If the museum is sponsoring a float in the parade—"

"Ooh! That could totally be it," George said eagerly. "Maybe it has to do with the contest Deirdre was yapping about. She made it sound like there would be big prizes for the winners—that probably means money."

Ned looked excited. "This could be our breakthrough, guys. I think we should go down there and check it out."

"You mean, to the museum?" I tilted my head in confusion. "But it's closed all weekend, remember?"

"No, not the museum," Ned replied. "All the floats are being built and stored in that big warehouse over on Sycamore Street—I had to fact-check the address last week for a little blurb in the Out and About section of the paper. We could go down there. Maybe . . ."

He didn't finish the sentence, but I did, if only in my own head: *Maybe Nancy is there!*

I shivered as I imagined Nancy bound and gagged in a warehouse full of huge, shadowy, silent floats. Believe it or not, the image actually cheered me up a little. It meant we might finally be about to find her!

"Come on." I pushed my coffee cup aside and jumped to my feet, suddenly filled with new energy. It's amazing what a little hope can do. "Let's go!"

"Is this it?" George's forehead wrinkled with confusion as she angled her car carefully, trying to squeeze around a large double-parked SUV that was taking up most of the street. "What's with all the traffic?"

I peered out the window with equal confusion. Far from being gloomy and deserted as I'd imagined, the place was positively bustling with activity. Cars were parked in every spare inch of space surrounding the huge, airplane-hangar-size building—in the parking lot, on the small strip of lawn between sidewalk and street, even in the lots of neighboring businesses. A pair of huge doors in the closest side of the building were flung wide open, and dozens of people rushed in and out carrying plywood, rolls of fabric, shopping bags, and all sorts of other stuff. Inside the warehouse I could just make out the large, weird-looking shapes of the parade floats.

"Wow," I said as George finally eased the car into an almost impossibly tiny open spot between a pickup truck and a lamppost. "I guess this is a big 'duh' on us, hmm? We probably should have known people would still be putting last-minute touches on their floats."

George just shrugged and frowned. She doesn't like admitting when she's missed something obvious. "Well, now that we're here, I guess we might as well go in and ask around a little," she said.

"Let's go." Ned was already easing open his door, trying not to scrape it on the metal lamppost only inches away. "At least here we'll have the opportunity to talk to a whole lot of people in a short amount of time. Maybe we can figure out if that parade note means anything."

As we walked toward the warehouse's entrance, dodging frantic float builders and haphazardly parked vehicles, I spotted a pretty young blond woman I recognized as a reporter from a local television station. Dressed in a stylish pink suit, she was speaking into a microphone and facing a cameraman.

"Check it out." I elbowed George. "Isn't that Stacey Kane from RH News? Maybe you can go get on TV."

"I think she's the one who did a report on Nancy's disappearance last night on the eleven o'clock news," Ned said. "My parents saw it."

"Really? Let's go talk to her." George turned and rushed toward the reporter.

"Hey!" Stacey Kane blurted out in surprise as George jumped into her shot. "Look out, we're trying to—hey, aren't you Nancy Drew's friend?"

I sighed, for a brief moment wondering if that was really all George, Ned, and I were to most people—*Nancy Drew's friends*. Quickly shaking off the irrelevant thought, I smiled at the reporter and the cameraman, who had lowered his camera and was staring at us curiously.

"That's right," I said. "We heard you did a report on Nancy last night, so we were just coming over to see if you guys had heard anything new."

George nodded vigorously. "Yeah," she said. "Any anonymous tips to the station, anything like that?"

"Sorry." The reporter smiled sympathetically. "I'm afraid if there's anything new, I haven't heard about it. I've been on the parade-prep beat since first thing this morning."

We thanked her and moved on toward the warehouse. When we reached the door, we saw that things were even busier inside than out. I just stood there for a moment in the doorway, watching as the incredible floats took shape right before our eyes. Just a few yards away several people were hoisting a glittering gold banner proclaiming their float to be the work of the First Bank of River Heights. Behind them at least a dozen kids were working frantically to staple streamers and flowers to the high school's enormous float. Off to one side I saw the animal shelter's smaller but more elaborately designed dog-shaped float, and near that was one shaped like a riverboat that seemed to be the product of the local historical society.

"Hey." I felt a sharp poke between my shoulder blades and George's hot breath on the back of my neck. "What are you waiting for? Let's get in there."

We plunged into the buzz of activity. Within seconds I'd lost track of both George and Ned, but I figured it didn't matter. We'd be able to cover more ground separately.

I spent the next half hour or so chatting with various float-building townspeople. Most of them were polite but distracted, clearly more interested in getting their floats finished in time than in helping me to solve my mystery. It wasn't easy to get anyone to focus on my questions for more than a moment or two, but when they did most of them were concerned but clueless. Nobody knew where Nancy might be, and nobody had seen her since Thursday at the latest. After about the twentieth or thirtieth apologetic shrug, I was starting to feel a little demoralized, but I smushed down that feeling and kept going, determined not to give up. Moving deeper and deeper into the warehouse, I did my best to question every person I could find. I even spent a few minutes helping several older women from the Mahoney Foundation hoist a large papier-mâché anvil onto their float just so they would have to talk to me.

It turns out that even papier-mâché anvils are heavy, and I was still panting slightly from the exertion as I moved on and spotted a float that I knew instantly had to be the one Deirdre had been so busy bragging about the last couple of times we'd seen her. It wasn't the largest float in the room, but one glance was all it took to know that it was the most expensive. Where most of the other floats relied on old standbys such as crepe paper and bunting, the Rackham Industries float was an elaborate, glittering mosaic of gold, jewels, and peacock feathers. The company's logo was spelled out in gold leaf in several spots, and live flowering shrubs and lily plants sprouted in gold-painted planters set around the edges of the float. But most astonishing of all was the enormous throne in the center, which appeared to be built entirely of computer chips, a symbol of the company's prominence in the computer industry. The throne's seat was padded with silk cushions and a worker was just carefully painting the current year on a banner overhead that already read MISS RACKHAM INDUSTRIES. All in all the float was quite a spectacle. I was standing there staring at it when George and Ned found me.

"Get anything good?" Ned asked.

I shook my head. "Afraid not," I told him apologetically. "Everyone was really sympathetic but had no idea where she could be. Oh, except that one of the ladies at the Garden League float suggested maybe Nancy secretly sneaked off to get plastic surgery."

George rolled her eyes. "Yeah, right," she said sarcastically. "That sounds just like Nancy."

"I haven't been getting much either," Ned admitted. "Not even at the police department float. But I just heard the university museum does have its own float, so I figured we should check that one out together."

It only took a few minutes to find our way to the

museum float. Like the museum itself, it was varied and interesting. Its sides were draped with posters showing reproductions of some of the museum's best-known paintings, while sculptures, local anthropology, Egyptian and other ancient artifacts, antique farm equipment, natural history, and other parts of the museum's diverse collection were represented by papier-mâché figures or other displays. About half a dozen people were working away busily on the float.

Ned collared an earnest-looking young woman with frizzy brown hair as she dashed past carrying a cardboard cutout of a Native American hut. "Excuse me," Ned said politely. "We have a question for you."

"Let me do the talking," George muttered out of the corner of her mouth, pushing her way past me and Ned. She stared intently at the frizzy-haired woman. "What's this we hear about a burglary at the museum?" she barked out.

The young woman looked startled. "A burglary at the museum?" she cried loudly. "When?"

A couple of other museum workers who were standing nearby overheard and turned toward us curiously. "What burglary?" they exclaimed. "What happened? What's going on?"

"Brilliant plan, Miss Holmes," I whispered to George. Clearing my throat, I addressed the group, which was growing as word spread. "Sorry about the confusion," I said. "We don't know about any actual burglary, but we heard something that made us think there might have been some trouble at the museum."

"That's right," Ned added. "Actually, we thought it might possibly have something to do with that visiting chess exhibit."

One of the workers, a young man wearing jeans so old and faded they looked as if they might disintegrate at any moment, rolled his eyes. "Yeah, right," he said. "Not with that crazy dog standing guard."

"Dog?" I repeated. "What dog?"

Suddenly all the gathered museum workers seemed eager to answer my question at once. For a second all I could make out were words and phrases here and there—"vicious beast," "two-foot fangs," "Cujo on steroids," and the like.

"A new guard dog?" George muttered in my ear. "Are you thinking what I'm thinking?"

I suspected that I was. As soon as the museum worker mentioned a guard dog, the first thing I'd thought of was our little encounter with Marge Kurz the day before. It wasn't long before we were able to confirm that connection.

"That's the lady," the frizzy-haired woman said with a nod when I mentioned Ms. Kurz's name. "She loaned ol' Killer to the museum free of charge for the whole time the chess exhibit is there."

After a few more questions, we left the museum people to their work and moved away. Coming across a relatively quiet spot between the back of the museum float and another float that already seemed to be finished, the three of us stopped to discuss what we'd just heard.

"Does anyone else think it's odd that Ms. Kurz is loaning out one of her dogs for free?" I asked.

Ned shrugged. "Not really," he said. "If she's new in town and trying to drum up business, it actually makes a lot of sense. If she gets herself a few satisfied customers, she should be able to expand her client list through word-of-mouth recommendations."

"Even so, it's not going to be easy for her to make a living in a city the size of River Heights," George predicted. "It's not like there's a huge call for specially trained guard dogs here. And since we already know how she feels about expanding her business to pet classes . . ."

I giggled, remembering Ms. Kurz's distaste at the subject. But George's next comment wiped the smile right back off my face.

"Unless, of course, Nancy never returns to keep crime at bay," she added darkly. "Then Ms. Kurz might be able to make a good living training guard dogs after all."

9

A New Connection

George

Bess and Ned actually seemed kind of excited with my ridiculous theory about the dog trainer. That left it to me to bring them back to earth.

"Look," I said matter-of-factly. "This is all very interesting, but get real. Nobody's going to commit a felony just to help herself hire out a few extra guard dogs, not even an obvious nut like that Kurz woman. And getting back to more reasonable theories, the truth is, we still have no idea whether or not there's been any kind of theft or other crime at the museum at all. Chess exhibit or otherwise."

Ned tapped his chin thoughtfully with one finger. "Okay, you're right. But maybe that's all part of the mystery. I mean, if there was a break-in or theft that has something to do with that chess exhibit—which seems like a logical sort of assumption—maybe there's a reason nobody seems to know about it. It could mean a lot of bad publicity for the museum if the news got out."

I furrowed my brow. "So what are you saying? That the museum kidnapped Nancy to keep her quiet?"

"Of course not," Ned said. "I'm saying that just because nobody we've talked to has heard about a problem at the museum, it doesn't mean it didn't happen."

Bess's eyes widened. "Oh! I have another idea," she exclaimed. "What if the theft, or whatever it is, hasn't happened yet? Maybe someone's trying to blackmail the museum somehow. Maybe even threatening to steal or harm that valuable chess set. And that's what Nancy heard about the other day."

"Well, that would certainly explain the guard dog, I guess." I was starting to think our theorizing was getting a little far-fetched. Then again, that was how I'd felt about most of our investigating so far. Solving a mystery isn't easy when you don't have a single solid clue to go on. Where were the footprints in the mud, the shadowy figure in the mist, the pasted-together ransom note? Then maybe we could get somewhere!

"I think it's time to get some real answers on this whole museum issue." Ned waved one hand at the museum staffers, who were already back at work on their float. "These people obviously don't know anything. It's time to go straight to the horse's mouth for some answers."

I couldn't help smirking a little as I realized who he meant. Valerie Abernathy, the director of the museum, really does look a little like a horse, with her long face, slightly droopy eyes, and oversize teeth.

"Good idea," I said, already turning toward the exit. "Let's motor, people. Time's awasting."

It's amazing how easy "mysteries" are to solve when the clues and leads turn up where they're supposed to and tell you what you need to know. We tracked down Valerie Abernathy by calling her house and talking to her daughter's teenage babysitter, who told us that Abernathy was "getting a facial." We then did yet more intricate sleuthing by calling various places in River Heights that offer such services, and voilà! Some twenty minutes later we were walking into the lobby of the newest and fanciest spa in the area, a full-service pore-cleansing, aura-stroking, vegetarian-food paradise called Indulgences. I'd heard it would be open on Sunday; apparently, it was true.

"What now?" Bess whispered as we crossed the airy, atriumlike lobby, heading toward the reception desk. "What if they won't let us in? Should we just hang out and wait for her?"

"That won't be necessary," I replied confidently. "Just leave it to me."

My mother's company had catered dozens of affairs at the museum, and I was sure that if I sent in an urgent message for Mrs. Abernathy, she'd at least be curious enough to see what it was about.

Sure enough, within minutes we were being ushered into a private room by a receptionist. Inside we found Mrs. Abernathy relaxing in a comfortable chair while a petite uniformed woman wiped grayish goo all over her face. The owner of the spa, a tall, attractive woman named Tessa Monroe, was also there chatting with Mrs. Abernathy. Bess and I stepped forward to say hello while Ned hung back by the door awkwardly, obviously trying not to notice that Mrs. Abernathy was dressed only in a terrycloth robe featuring the spa's logo.

Fortunately he seemed to be the only one feeling uncomfortable. "Why, hello, girls," Mrs. Abernathy greeted us with a smile. "Where's Nancy?"

I hid a grimace. This time I hadn't expected it— Mrs. Abernathy is probably one of the few people in town who knows Nancy as a friend of mine rather than the other way around.

Luckily Bess was there to step in with a polite answer. "That's sort of the reason we're here," she told the two women. Well, three women counting the facialist, or whatever she would be called, though she gave no glimmer of interest in our conversation as she continued slopping her goo onto Mrs. A's face. "Nancy has been missing for going on three days now, and we . . ."

I sort of faded out on the rest of Bess's explanation, suddenly struck by those five little words: *going on three days now.* Had it really been that long? My gut was seized by a little spasm of panic. Three days was too long. Way too long. There was no way that anyone—not even Bess—could pretend that there wasn't something shady going on. The question was, would we be able to figure it out before it was too late? It sure didn't feel likely at the moment, given that we were no closer to any answers than we'd been on that first day. . . .

Meanwhile Tessa and Mrs. Abernathy were giving the usual little exclamations of shock and asking the usual questions. "Do the police have any leads?" Mrs. Abernathy inquired at one point.

Ned overcame his male-pattern spa-averse shyness enough to step forward. "Not that we're aware of," he said. "That's why we're trying to puzzle out what might have happened. Right now we're trying to figure out the meaning of an e-mail Nancy sent out shortly before she disappeared, which mentioned your museum." He nodded toward Mrs. Abernathy.

The museum director looked surprised. "The museum? What about it?"

"She seemed to think there might be some trouble going on there," I spoke up. "Maybe a theft or something?"

"Or a threatened theft," Bess added.

Mrs. Abernathy shook her head, almost bumping into the facial lady's glop wand or whatever it's called. "I don't know what she could have meant," she said. "There's been no trouble at the museum lately." She glanced over at the spa owner and sighed. "Well, aside from my staff being all in a tizzy over this chess exhibit, of course. I was just complaining to Tessa about that when you came in."

"What do you mean?" Ned asked.

"Oh, it's silly, really." Mrs. Abernathy sighed again. "My senior staff is a bit worried about this chess exhibit. We don't get that many traveling exhibits here—most of the high-profile shows bypass us and end up at one of the bigger museums in Chicago—and so we're not really used to having such valuable things on loan."

"But there are tons of valuable things at the museum all the time," Bess pointed out. "Why, that statue in the lobby alone must be worth tons. And then there's the painting the Mahoney Foundation raised money to buy you last spring, and those rare books Morris

99

Granger donated from his private collection. . . ."

"You're right, of course, my dear." The museum director nodded. "The museum is fortunate enough to own plenty of really lovely and valuable things—paintings, artifacts, antique furniture, and household items—many of them kindly donated by some of the wealthier citizens of River Heights. But that's different, somehow, than being responsible for the priceless property of others. And I'm afraid our security system is a bit of a museum piece itself—quite antiquated, really." She blew out her lips in a loud sigh, accidentally shaking loose some of the crusty gray mud on her upper lip. "Why Rackham Industries will pay out big bucks for a silly float, but not donate to something for the educational good of the community, I'll never understand. . . ."

I raised one eyebrow curiously, shooting a quick glance at my friends. "Rackham Industries?" I asked the woman. "What do they have to do with this?"

The museum director laughed, looking sheepish. "Oh, don't mind me," she said. "There's no reason in particular why the company should donate to our security fund. I just wish they would. Then we wouldn't have to rely on extra security guards, human and canine, to protect things."

"Speaking of canines, we just heard about your new guard dog from Ms. Kurz," Ned commented.

"Yes, well, that's only temporary," Mrs. Abernathy said. "I'm sure Ms. Kurz is hoping we'll keep her pooch on even after the exhibit moves on, but as I've told her repeatedly, it's just not in our budget." She glanced over at the spa owner. "Perhaps Tessa can use the poor critter when he's done with us."

Tessa chuckled. "I'm not sure my customers would appreciate that."

I narrowed my eyes slightly, detecting an overly amused glance traveling between the two women. "So you're not pleased with this guard dog, then?" I asked Mrs. Abernathy.

"Oh, it's not that, Georgia," Mrs. Abernathy assured me, looking slightly surprised at my pointed question. Oops. "The creature is undoubtedly very well-trained. Not to mention effective. Nobody is getting past that thing." A ghost of a smile played across her lips. "Why, it's even scaring away half my staff."

Ned and Bess went on to ask a few more questions about the chess exhibit and other things, but I wasn't really paying attention. I had a feeling we were missing something here. We had a lot of information now, and some of it even seemed to be pointing to some interesting connections. But what did any of it mean when it came to Nancy? I would have given a million-dollar chess set for one of her famous hunches at that moment.

When I tuned back in, Mrs. Abernathy was talking about her security system again. "And anytime the power goes out, the entire system has to be reset by hand. As Tommy and Zane like to say, it's like some kind of huge, expensive old clock radio."

"Zane?" I repeated, wondering why that name sounded so familiar. "Wait! You're not talking about Zane Quinn, are you?"

Once again the woman seemed startled by my interrogatory tone. "Why, yes," she said cautiously. "Do you know him?"

"Not exactly," I said, trying not to let her see how excited I was. If this Zane Quinn was the ex-convict who had so recently e-mailed Nancy, that meant he was now working at the museum—the very museum where Nancy thought something suspicious might be happening. Talk about an interesting connection! "But, um, we really want to talk to him. Can you give us his address?"

"His address? Why would you need that?"

I didn't want to blurt out, "Because he's the nasty, lowdown ex-con scumbag who kidnapped our friend!" So instead, I said, "Er, I think I went to summer camp with him back in elementary school."

"Really?" Mrs. Abernathy blinked. "How odd. I'm quite sure he's at least ten years older than you girls."

"Counselor," I blurted out, ignoring Bess's expression, which was wavering somewhere between amused and horrified. "Er, he was a counselor at my camp. That's what I meant to say."

"Oh." She looked a little confused by that, but she was too polite to say anything. "Well, I'm afraid it's against our policy to give out personal information about museum employees without their express permission." The museum director's voice was kind but firm. "I'm very sorry, Georgia, but I can't make an exception, even for you."

"Oh. Um, okay." Once again I found myself desperately missing Nancy, who had the uncanny ability to get the information she needed out of practically anybody. "Er, but I feel like I should warn you, I think Quinn has been in jail—"

"I'm well aware of that, young lady." The woman's voice took on a rather sharp, scolding tone. "I'm also well aware that young Zane is one of the best hires I've made recently. He's paid his debt to society, and I trust him implicitly. I also trust no one will be spreading any sort of gossip about his past around town."

It wasn't really phrased as a question, but I nodded and smiled weakly. "Sorry," I mumbled. "Just wanted to make sure you know."

Since it was pretty obvious at that point that we

weren't going to get any more useful information out of Mrs. Abernathy, we took the first opportunity to excuse ourselves. Outside the mud-goop room, we paused for a quick conference.

"Nice going in there, George," Ned said with a grin. "Very smooth. Very tactful."

"Shut up, Nickerson," I muttered.

"Zane Quinn," Bess said eagerly. "That's the guy who sent Nancy the e-mail, right?"

"And now he's working at the museum," Ned mused. "That can't be a coincidence, can it?"

"It is sort of weird," Bess said. "How come he's out of jail early? How did he end up working at the museum, of all places? And why did he e-mail Nancy just a couple of days before she disappeared?"

I was already heading for the exit. "We won't know the answers until we find Quinn!"

10

Running Out of Time

Bess

You know," George said, "when they show stake-outs on TV or in the movies, they never look nearly this boring."

I glanced over at her with a sympathetic smile. George, Ned, and I had been sitting in George's car for the past hour and a half. It had taken longer than we'd expected to figure out where Zane Quinn lived—he wasn't listed in the phone directory, and a simple Internet search hadn't turned up anything at first. George had finally managed to pull the information out of her laptop, though I didn't ask her exactly how. I wasn't sure I wanted to know.

In any case we'd eventually found Quinn's tiny rented house, which was located on a sleepy side street in Muskoka Valley, a low-income neighborhood of older ranch homes and small apartment buildings on the south side of town. There were a few other cars parked along the curb, and we'd found a spot a short distance down the block to avoid looking conspicuous.

We needn't have worried. In all the time we'd been watching, only two people had wandered past—the mail carrier and an elderly woman walking a miniature poodle.

"Where the heck is he?" George muttered, glancing irritably from the front door of Quinn's house to the clock in the car's dashboard.

Ned yawned and stretched as best he could in the backseat. As tall as he was, it had to be even harder on him than on us to sit in the cramped car for so long. "I don't know," he said. "But I'm starting to wonder if we're wasting our time here. Time we don't have to waste," he added pointedly.

I bit my lip, knowing he was right. It was Sunday afternoon. Nancy had gone missing on Friday morning. That was a long time. Way too long to think about it very hard, or I would get too upset to focus on finding her.

"Maybe you're right," I said after a moment. "Maybe we should give up here; we could tell the police what we found out and let them check up on Quinn while we—"

"Shhh!" George hissed, suddenly bolting forward

in her seat and grasping the edge of the dashboard, peering out eagerly through the windshield. "Check it out—someone's coming!"

"Is it Zane?" Ned asked, leaning forward and trying to see where George was looking.

I'd just spotted the figure wandering up the weedy front walk of Quinn's house. "I don't think that's him," I said. "Unless he turned into a woman while he was in jail."

"Very funny." George was already opening the car door. "Come on, let's go talk to her. She must know him, or she wouldn't be going up to his house, right?"

I shrugged and climbed out of the car, hoping we weren't about to descend on some hapless meter reader or Jehovah's Witness. The young woman turned as she heard the three of us stampeding toward her. A wan-looking young woman of about twenty-five with lank brown hair, she was wearing an unfortunate outfit of oversize denim shorts and a ratty tank top. A key ring dangled from one hand.

"Excuse us," I said, smiling brightly to reassure her that we meant her no harm. "We're looking for Mr. Quinn. Do you know where he is?"

"Zane?" The young woman gave her head a single violent shake to fling a chunk of hair out of her face. She stared at us suspiciously. "He's not here."

"We can see that," George said, her voice tight and impatient.

Shooting her a warning look, Ned took a step forward. "It's really important for us to talk with him soon," he told the young woman politely, giving her a smile that would make most females over the age of twelve swoon on the spot. "Please, do you know when he'll be home?"

"Who are you guys, anyway?" She still looked wary.

I quickly told her our first names. "Are you a friend of Mr. Quinn's?" I asked.

"I live over there." She waved one hand limply in the general direction of another house on the block. "Zane asked me to take in the mail and feed his cat while he's gone."

"Gone?" George repeated sharply. "Gone where?"

"Dunno." The neighbor shrugged. "But he'll be away for a while. Until that dang dog is gone, he said."

"Dog?" I wrinkled my forehead in confusion, flashing back to the little poodle we'd watched prance past the car half an hour earlier.

Luckily Ned was a little more on the ball. "You mean the guard dog at the museum?" he asked. His voice remained calm and even, but I knew him well enough to see the glint of excitement in his eyes.

"Yeah, that's the one." The neighbor shifted the keys to her other hand. "Zane isn't real big on dogs.

'Specially big mean ones like that. Said it was, you know, a hostile work environment or something. Took off to stay with his folks until it's gone—oh yeah, think he said they're in Phoenix. Anyway, it means he won't be back until that chess thing leaves in a couple weeks, I guess." The young woman rolled her eyes. "Told him he was being dumb. Now he won't have any more vacation time until next year."

The young woman had apparently decided we were safe to talk to, because she started rambling on about the limited vacation time at her own job. Meanwhile my friends and I were staring at one another in shock. Quinn was out of town? If that was true, our whole new lead had just gone spiraling down the drain!

We managed to extricate ourselves from Quinn's suddenly talkative neighbor and hurried back to the car. As George started the engine, there was a long moment of silence. I guess we were all feeling a little deflated.

"Well," Ned said at last. "So much for that."

"Maybe she was lying," I suggested, trying to look for the bright side. "Covering for him or something. Or maybe he took Nancy with him when he left town."

"I guess that's possible," Ned said doubtfully. "We forgot to ask her *when* he left town."

I glanced out the window. The young woman had already disappeared into Quinn's house. "I could run over and ask her."

"I have a better idea." George cut the engine again. "Hand me my laptop."

I passed her the computer that was nestled at my feet. George isn't quite so computer-obsessed that she brings it with her absolutely everywhere, but today she'd decided it might come in handy.

Using the wireless modem on which she'd spent most of her birthday money, she quickly connected to the Internet. As she went to work, I leaned back against the seat and stared out at Quinn's house, thinking about what we'd just learned. Did Quinn really have anything to do with Nancy's disappearance, or was it just a wild-goose chase? I really wasn't sure, and that made me uneasy. As much as I was trying to keep my own spirits up, along with those of my friends, solving this mystery was starting to feel like putting together a picture with pieces from eight or nine different puzzles. We were finding out what seemed like interesting bits of information, but none of them seemed to go together in any useful way. More importantly, none of them seemed to be leading us any closer to Nancy. . . .

"Got it," George said, interrupting my thoughts. "Found airline reservations for a Z. Quinn, departing from O'Hare in Chicago and arriving in Phoenix."

"When?" Ned asked tensely.

George peered at the screen. "Departure date . . . oh." She shrugged. "Last Friday afternoon."

I sighed. "Oh, well," I said. "Guess that's one suspect we can cross off the list, then. There's no way he could have kidnapped Nancy Friday morning and still had time to get to Chicago, right?"

"Unless he didn't make that flight," Ned argued halfheartedly. "Or just drove really fast . . ."

George logged off and snapped the computer shut. "Come on," she said heavily. "Let's get out of here."

While she pulled away from the curb, I took out my phone. "I'm going to call Chief McGinnis and tell him what we found out about Quinn," I said. "Just in case."

"Good idea," Ned said. "Maybe they can check on whether he's really in Phoenix like he's supposed to be."

I dialed the number for the police station. After just one ring, a brisk female voice answered. "River Heights Police Department. How may I help you?"

"Hi, Tonya," I said, recognizing her voice. Tonya Ward has been the receptionist at the police station for a long time. She's always been a good friend to Nancy, helping her out whenever she could. Luckily, she was working—probably because it was a holiday weekend. "It's Bess Marvin. How are you?"

"Bess." Tonya's crisp, businesslike voice softened. "How are you holding up? The chief has been going all out trying to find Nancy."

"That's great." Her words actually made me feel a little better. After interrupting the chief at his barbecue yesterday, I'd wondered if he was really taking Nancy's disappearance seriously enough. But if Tonya said he was on the case, I knew it was true. "We just checked out a possible lead, and I was hoping to fill him in. Is he there?"

"I'll get him."

I glanced over at George and Ned as I waited. "Sounds like the chief is really getting serious about this now," I told them. "That's good, right? He'll probably find her soon."

They didn't answer. Just then the chief came on the line. "Miss Marvin?" he said breathlessly. "Tonya tells me you have some news."

"Well, maybe not news exactly . . ." I told him what we'd found out about Zane Quinn.

"Hmm," he said when I finished. "All right, I'll have someone check and make sure he's still in Phoenix. But we'd already crossed Quinn off the suspect list this morning when the airline confirmed he was on that flight. Alone. We even checked out his house earlier just in case. Nobody there."

"Oh." I couldn't help feeling kind of stupid. It

seemed the police were way ahead of us on this angle, which meant we'd just wasted a couple of hours on nothing.

The chief was still chattering into my ear. "We're still searching the local farms and other areas near town in case she just fell and got hurt somewhere, but we're also in touch with stations in neighboring cities, and even Chicago. We've also got a squad car staking out her house, and I just talked to Carson about tapping their home phone just in case. Ransom, you know."

I could tell he was worried if he was telling me so much. Usually he's not exactly eager to share the details of police work with amateurs, even Nancy. "Thanks, Chief," I said, trying to sound more cheerful than I felt. "We're going to keep poking around too."

"Well, I suppose I know better than to advise you to stay out of it." Though his words were gruff, his voice was surprisingly kind. "But be careful, all right? We don't really know what we're dealing with here, and I don't want anyone hurt."

"Okay. 'Bye." I hung up and told my friends what he'd said.

"Wow," Ned said. "Sounds like he's really thinking kidnapping now."

"Well, I don't know what good it's going to do to tap her phone and stuff." George sounded frustrated. "If someone was going to call for ransom they would

113

have done it by now. And staking out her house? Come on—talk about closing the barn door after the horse is out!"

"I'm sure the police are just trying to cover all the bases," I pointed out quietly. "Just like we're trying to do by following up all these sketchy leads. They probably don't have any more idea where she might be than we do. After all, there's no obvious motive or suspect. . . ."

"So what are we all missing?" Ned asked, sounding a little desperate. "There's got to be something, some clue or motive we haven't figured out yet. . . ."

I sighed, rubbing my temples as if that might jump-start my brain. It didn't work. Nancy's disappearance made no more sense than ever.

"It's going to be dark soon, and we aren't getting anywhere," Ned said anxiously. "Tomorrow's going to be a madhouse around town, what with the parade and everything. I'm supposed to cover the parade for the paper, and at least half the police department will be busy directing traffic and keeping order. . . ."

"I know." I took a deep breath, trying to summon up whatever was left of my optimistic spirit. "That's why we've got to find Nancy tonight!"

11

Another Stakeout

George

O kay, guys," I said, pulling my car to a stop at the side of the street. We'd just returned from our fruitless trip to Zane Quinn's house and were back downtown. Union Street, to be exact—that was as far as I felt like driving without a plan, since we were only a few blocks from River Street and the last thing we needed was to get snarled in the Independence Day Festival traffic. "So what are we going to do now?" Ever since Bess's proclamation about having to find Nancy that night, we'd all been mostly silent, thinking our own thoughts about just how we were supposed to do that.

Ned was ready with an answer, sort of. "We need to stop running around following random whims," he said firmly. "I think we should just pick out our most

115

solid lead or clue or whatever and go from there."

My first thought was that this wasn't how Nancy would do it. If she wasn't having any luck with the clues at hand, she would cast a wider net, not limit her options further. Then again, Nancy wasn't here. . . .

"Makes sense," Bess agreed. "So what's our most solid lead or clue?"

I knew the answer to that one. "The museum," I said confidently. "That's what Nancy's e-mail was about. That's also the focus, sort of, of the whole weird chess connection—the meeting on her calendar, the valuable exhibit. Even the Zane Quinn thing, in case that means anything."

Bess nodded. "Good point."

Ned shook his head. "I don't know," he said. "I still keep coming back to the park. That's the last place anyone saw Nancy. There has to be a clue there somewhere."

"Oh! That's a good point too," Bess said.

"Make up your mind." I rolled my eyes. "We can't investigate two places at once."

"Sure we can," Bess replied logically. "There are three of us. Maybe we should split up and stake out both places."

I groaned. "Another stakeout? Do we have to?"

"If we want to find Nancy, I guess we do," Ned replied.

That shut me up fast. At least in terms of complaining. At least for the moment. "Okay," I said. "So is that the plan? We're going to split up?"

"It makes sense." Ned glanced out the window at the sky, which was beginning to go pink with the approaching sunset. "It's getting late, so you two girls had better stick together."

I was going to make a sarcastic comment about him acting like Mr. Macho, but I thought better of it. For one thing, I didn't want to wind up staking out a deserted park or empty museum on my own while Bess and Ned stuck together. "Okay," I said. "We'll take the museum and you can check out the park. Do you have your cell phone?"

Ned patted his pocket. "Right here," he said. "I'll call if I see anything suspicious, and you do the same."

"Deal." I started the car again. "We'll drop you off on our way to the museum."

After a quick pit stop at a fast-food place for takeout, Bess and I dropped off Ned at the entrance to Anvil Park. There were still quite a few people there enjoying the mild summer evening.

"Good luck," I told him as he stepped out of the backseat.

"Thanks. Good luck to you guys too. And be careful."

I watched as he loped off toward an empty bench just inside the park entrance. "Ready?" Bess said from her seat beside me. "Let's get going."

It was a short drive to the museum. Passing the entrance to the small parking lot, I found a free spot on the street nearby. "We don't want to raise suspicions by being the only car in the lot," I pointed out, proud of my own reasoning there. It was just the type of thing Nancy would think of, I told myself.

"Yes," Bess said, "but that means we won't be able to watch from the car. You can't see the front entrance from here."

She was right. In fact, our view of most of the building was blocked by a hedge and a couple of sizable trees.

"True," I said, pulling the key out of the ignition. "But a bad guy isn't going to go waltzing up the front steps anyway. We should try to find a good hiding spot near the back entrance."

Bess shivered. "It's weird to be doing this kind of thing without Nancy, isn't it?"

I didn't answer. We climbed out of the car and I locked the doors. There's usually not much crime around the university, but I wasn't about to take any chances, especially with my computer in the car.

We pushed our way through a hole in the hedge and wandered around behind the museum building for a few minutes. There was only one entrance back there, a glass-paneled door labeled STAFF ONLY. It was locked, but by peering through the age-clouded glass I could see that it led into a long, stark hallway lit by a single bare bulb.

"Come on, let's hunker down over there." I gestured to a clump of bushes nearby.

Bess nodded, following me with our bags of food. "Are we sure this is a good idea?" she fretted. "Even if the museum mystery has some connection with Nancy's disappearance, how likely is it, really, that someone might decide to break in here tonight of all nights?"

"Quit second-guessing the plan now." I shot her an irritated look. Why had her famous optimism chosen this particular moment to desert her? "We're here, we might as well stick around for a while and see what happens. It's not like we have any other brilliant ideas."

"Okay, okay. Just asking."

We crawled into the middle of the bushes, where there was a small, almost cozy clearing. The leaves surrounding us were thick enough to hide us from passersby, but sparse enough to offer us a pretty good view of the back entrance.

"Perfect," Bess said happily, settling herself down on the bare dirt.

That wasn't quite the word I would have chosen myself. But I agreed that the spot would do for our purposes.

It only took a few minutes to eat our greasy burgers and fries and suck down our sodas. When we were finished, Bess got up and took our trash out to the bin on the sidewalk. Then we just sat there watching the ants crawling across the dirt in front of us, and the squirrels playing in the treetops overhead.

After about twenty minutes of that, I was already starting to go a little stir crazy. "Hey," I said quietly. "Maybe we shouldn't just sit here, you know? We could sort of, like, you know, patrol a little bit every once in a while. Sort of sneak around the perimeter of the building, see if anyone's hanging around or whatever."

"Okay," Bess replied. "I guess that wouldn't hurt. But one of us should probably stay here just in case we miss something." She waved a hand toward the back door.

"Fine. You hang here. I'll be right back."

I hopped to my feet and carefully eased out of our hiding place, relieved to be moving again. Honestly, I didn't really think I was going to see anything useful by wandering around the building. But it was better than sitting there all night letting my behind become one with the ground.

I took my time making my rounds, but my trek around the museum only took a few minutes even though I was being careful and keeping to the shadows as much as possible. Slowing down as I neared our hiding spot again, I took one last look around. The sky overhead was starting to go sort of fuzzy with a hint of twilight, and the streetlights had come on, their glow looking pale and watery in the remaining daylight. The museum building stood impassively overlooking the little yard where we were hiding, nothing moving other than a pigeon or two walking around on the roof.

Bess looked up as I slid back in and sat down next to her. "Anything?"

"Nope."

We repeated the same process several times over the next hour or two as the light faded completely and the hum of crickets took over from the twittering of birds. It was boring. Really boring. Mind-numbingly, spirit-crushingly boring. But each time I felt like giving up and going home to watch TV, I thought about Nancy. Wherever she was, she had to be scared and wondering when she would ever get home again. That kept me sitting there in the dark. I didn't know if what we were doing would help bring her home. But it had to be better than giving up.

As we sat there, Bess and I would occasionally

discuss the case for a while in low tones. But that got pretty boring too, since neither of us was coming up with anything new based on the facts at hand.

I don't know what time it was when I stood up and prepared for another trip around the building, though it was fully dark by then. "Be right back," I told Bess.

Once again I crawled out of our hiding place and headed around the side of the building. There was hardly any traffic in the area and almost no one on the street, either—the museum was on campus, and it seemed that just about everyone at the university had either cleared out for the holiday, or was still over at the festival. It was so quiet where we were that as I rounded the corner by the street, where the sound of the crickets faded slightly, I could hear the distant sound of an oompah band playing way over on River Street. I found myself listening as I made my rounds outside the building, and wishing that Bess and I were over there goofing off and eating greasy festival food with Nancy instead of sitting around on the damp ground staring at nothing.

Then I caught myself. Again. As long as Nancy remained missing, I wouldn't stop until—

A sudden, muffled sound came from somewhere very close by, interrupting my thoughts. I stopped short, listening with every ounce of concentration I possessed. Was I hearing things, or had that come from the direction of the museum?

I turned slowly to face the building. It looked huge and shadowy in the secondhand glow from the streetlights. I stared bug-eyed at its impressive facade, not daring to move a muscle.

Clunk. Thump.

There it was again! It sounded muted and sort of tinny, sort of like listening to someone banging around repairing a water pipe or something from another floor of a building. Or perhaps, I told myself, like someone trying to break into a valuable museum exhibit . . . My heart started pounding. Could this be what we were waiting for?

I was debating whether to run back and tell Bess or pull out my phone and call Ned or the police when I heard another muffled sound:

Woof!

My whole body suddenly relaxed. "Never mind," I muttered under my breath. "Just the stupid guard dog."

I'd almost forgotten about good old Killer, as the museum workers had (jokingly, I hoped) called him. Now that I remembered, the dog's presence made it seem even less likely that anyone would try to break into the building that night. But like I'd told Bess, it was too late to second-guess the plan now.

I hurried back to the hiding spot and told Bess

what I'd heard. "I thought I heard a bark too," she said. "I couldn't tell if it was coming from the museum or somewhere else, though."

"It was definitely coming from the museum."

We returned to our task of sitting there doing nothing. If there's anything that defines "opposite of exciting" better than staking out some guy's house during the day, it's staking out an empty building at night.

An undetermined amount of time passed. I was almost dozing off when a sudden shrill tone snapped me back to full attention.

Bess let out a little squeak. "What's that?" she cried, sitting bolt upright.

I grabbed my phone out of my pocket. "Sorry," I said. "I meant to put it on vibrate."

It was Ned calling us to check in. "Anything to report?" he asked.

"Not really," I replied. "We heard ol' Killer rustling around inside, but that's it."

"Killer?" Ned sounded confused.

"The guard dog. Remember?"

"Oh, right." Ned sighed. "Nothing much happening here, either. Everybody cleared out about an hour ago, and since then it's just been me and the mosquitoes."

I winced on his behalf. At least the shrubbery seemed to be protecting Bess and me from the throngs of biting insects that were everyone's least favorite parts of every midwestern summer. "Bummer," I said. "Do you want us to come pick you up?"

"Not a chance." Ned sounded tired but determined. "Now that I'm here, I might as well stick it out."

I wasn't sure that was the most logical way of approaching a plan, but I had to agree with him. "Same here," I told him. "It's not like bad guys work nine to five, right?"

We hung up, and I switched my phone ringer to vibrate. Then I told Bess what Ned had said.

"We might be wasting our time," I admitted. "But hey, at least if someone tries anything funny here or at the park tonight, we'll be there to see it. And maybe that'll be the break we need to find Nancy."

Of course, we weren't likely to see anything at all if we wound up falling asleep on our stakeout. All the worrying I'd been doing over the past three days was awfully tiring, and I found myself yawning about every fifteen seconds. Bess didn't look much more alert than I felt.

Trying to wake myself up a little, I went out for another patrol. It was quieter than ever; even the distant oompah band had fallen silent, and I guessed that the party was breaking up over on River Street. A few more muffled thumps and clangs emerged from inside the museum, but I ignored them. I was pretty sure nobody had gotten past us to the door, which meant it was surely just Killer moving around in there looking for somebody to chomp.

I lingered as long as I could on my rounds. When I returned, Bess was snoring softly. Nudging her awake, I gave her my report, such as it was.

"And watch it," I told her sternly as I sat down. "We can't fall asleep, okay?"

"Okay," she said thickly, stifling a yawn.

That set me yawning too. I shifted around, trying to find a comfortable part of the shrub's gnarled trunk so I could lean back against it. In a few minutes I would do another patrol, but first I just needed to rest my eyes for a moment. . . .

The next thing I knew, I was yanked rudely out of a sound sleep by the sound of wild barking.

12

A Bungled Break-In

Bess

Wha—buh—huh?" **George** stammered as she sat up suddenly, almost banging her head into mine.

I rubbed my eyes and stared around in the near dark, for a moment not knowing where I was or what was going on. Then the loud flurry of barking came again.

"Killer," I gasped, realizing we'd both fallen sound asleep. "Wha-what's he barking at in there?"

George was already lurching to her feet. "Come on, let's go check it out!"

"Wait!" I blurted out, my mind still fuzzy with sleep. "George, be careful!" It had to be after midnight by then, though I couldn't see my watch in the dark. I didn't want to try to imagine what kind of commotion could be causing Killer to bark his head off like that.

I pushed my way out of our hiding place and almost bumped into George, who was frozen at the edge of the shrubbery. "Shhh," she hissed. "Do you hear footsteps?"

Before I could answer, the back door of the museum suddenly crashed open. A shadowy figure dashed out, cursing and shouting. The barking suddenly got louder, and my eyes widened as I saw an enormous dog—Killer—burst into view just inside. The shadowy figure spun and slammed the door shut just in time; a split second later came the loud thud of the dog's heavy body crashing into the door. The barking continued, sounding angrier and more frantic than ever.

The mysterious figure was still standing outside the door. It was too dark in the shadows of the building to get a good look, or even to tell if the stranger was a man or a woman. I melted back into the bushes, wondering what we should do now.

I gasped as George marched forward. "Hey!" she shouted. "You there!"

"George!" I whispered frantically. "What are you doing?"

I'm not someone who lets her imagination run wild along the dark side of life very often, but at that moment my head was filled with Technicolor visions of several possible outcomes of George's reckless action, most of them violent or at least fairly unpleasant. Fortunately none of them came to pass. Instead the figure jumped, letting out a cry of surprise. "Who's there?"

This time I was pretty sure it was a man's voice. I squinted as George hurried forward, willing my eyes to see through the darkness. A moment later I heard my cousin call my name.

"It's okay, you can come out," she added. "It's just Mr. Pembleton."

I blinked in astonishment, then slowly walked over to join them. At first I was still cautious—Marcus Pembleton had always seemed like a nice, perfectly harmless man. But thanks to my many adventures with Nancy, I'd seen an awful lot of seemingly nice, harmless people do surprising things when they felt cornered or desperate.

Once I got a better look at the man's pale, terrified face, though, I started to feel a little more confident. He didn't look shifty-eyed or frantic at all. If anything, he seemed sort of glad to see us.

"Oh, girls," he exclaimed breathlessly. "Did you see that terrible creature in there? Why, I hesitate even to call it a dog! Dogs love me! But that beast . . ."

His voice trailed off in a sort of verbal shudder,

and he shook his head. Meanwhile I had just noticed that he was holding something, dangling it loosely from one hand.

"What were you doing in there?" George asked him sternly.

I pointed to the item he was holding, wondering if he'd managed to snatch something from inside the museum despite Killer's best efforts. "And what's that?" I added.

Mr. Pembleton looked sheepish as he held up the item, which turned out to be a large plastic bag full of raw meat. "Oh, well, I suppose I'm busted," he said, not sounding nearly as upset as most people might in a similar situation. He sighed sadly and ran his free hand through his thinning gray hair. "I know it was foolish—I just couldn't resist, I'm afraid. I'm a weak man."

George held up both hands. "Hold on," she said. "This is all too weird. What in the world are you doing here? Why were you in the museum? And why do you have that meat?"

I was starting to figure out some possible answers to that myself. But I waited to hear what the man had to say.

Mr. Pembleton winced as Killer flung himself against the inside of the door again. The dog was still barking nonstop.

"Well, the meat was supposed to be for him." He hooked a thumb in the direction of the noisy dog. "See, I heard he was guarding the chess exhibit at night, but I figured all dogs think with their stomachs, right?" He shook his head. "Thought I'd toss him a nice, juicy steak, give him a pat on the head, and he'd give me no trouble at all. Dogs usually love me!"

I exchanged a quick glance with George. Mr. Pembleton might love dogs, but he didn't seem to understand them quite as well as he thought. Of course, anyone who'd ever seen Rufus dragging him around would realize that.

"Okay," I said. "But why did you want to get into the museum in the first place?"

"It was that chess set." He sighed, glancing wistfully over his shoulder at the museum. "I'm sure you've heard about it—the one from ancient India? Of course, it's actually not technically a chess set at all. It's more of a precursor to modern chess that was known at that time as *Chaturanga*. Very, very rare indeed!"

George nodded. "I see," she said. "So you planned to steal this chess set—er, or Chata–whatever, I mean—and sell it on the black market or something?"

I realized that made perfect sense. Everybody in town knew that Mr. Pembleton always felt like he didn't have enough money.

The man looked slightly insulted. "Of course not! I only wanted it for my own collection." He sighed again. "Oh, I know it was wrong. It just seemed so easy, so tempting, with only that dog and the museum's pathetic excuse for a security system standing in front of me. . . . Besides," he added, his expression darkening slightly, "if I didn't take it, it wouldn't be safe in River Heights for long, and then who knows where it might end up."

"Huh? What do you mean?" George asked.

The man sighed, his angry expression crumpling and leaving him looking tired and timeworn. "Never mind," he murmured. "Now, I'm sure you young ladies are going to want to do the right thing and call the police, yes? You might as well go ahead now before it gets any later."

I couldn't help feeling a little bit sorry for him. He had always seemed like such a nice, mild-mannered man. A man who cared about his abandoned dogs, his rundown farm, and his cherished collections. I guess he cared about the last part a little too much.

George didn't seem nearly so sympathetic. "Fine," she said, pulling out her cell phone. "I'll call right now. I'm sure Chief McGinnis will be happy to talk to you."

For the next ten or fifteen minutes, while waiting

for the police to arrive, we finally had the chance to ask Mr. Pembleton about Nancy. Sadly, he seemed genuinely puzzled by our questions.

"Is she still missing? Oh, dear," he said. "But you asked me about her already, remember? At the festival?"

"Yes, but . . ." George shot me a confused glance. "Well, we just thought you might have remembered something, that's all," she added lamely.

Recalling the way Nancy herself often tripped up people who didn't want to confess to something by asking them questions about something else, I tried to get Mr. Pembleton to say more about the chess set he'd been trying to pilfer. But he no longer seemed to be in a talkative mood. He politely insisted on waiting to say anything more until he'd consulted his attorney.

As the gleam of red and blue flashing lights appeared in the distance, I just stood there beside the others, waiting for the squad car to reach us. Now that the rush of adrenaline had worn off, I felt limp and perplexed. Wasn't this supposed to be our big moment, the moment when the bad guy confesses to everything?

Soon several police officers were bustling around, checking the scene, calling the museum manager to notify her, and of course taking poor Mr. Pembleton into custody. George had also called Ned, who showed up just seconds behind the squad car, panting from jogging the whole way.

"Well?" He huffed and puffed as he rushed over to us. "Did he tell you where Nancy is?"

"No, sorry," I said, the answer to his question settling in my gut like a lead weight. We had solved one mystery—presumably the one Nancy had referenced in that e-mail—but the more important one was still open.

Where was Nancy?

13

Museum Musings

George

Ugh," I grumbled as yet another person brushed past me, almost knocking me into Bess. "Can't people watch where they're going?"

Bess glanced over at me. "They don't mean anything by it, they're just excited and not watching where they're going," she reminded me. "They're all just here to have a good time and watch the parade."

Leave it to Bess to make excuses for random rude strangers. I was about to open my mouth and say something sarcastic, but then I took a closer look at my cousin and kept quiet.

Bess looked terrible. And let me tell you, that's not a sentence you'll hear every day. My cousin is one of those rare people who could chase a warthog through a mud puddle and still come out the other end flower-fresh and perfectly pressed, with every blond hair in place and not a speck of dirt on her clothes. It's downright irritating at times.

But today I noticed there were a couple of obvious chips in her pink nail polish. Her hair was tied back in a sloppy ponytail and looked as if it hadn't been washed that morning. And there were some serious dark circles under her blue eyes, indicating that she probably hadn't slept any more than I had the past few days. That was really saying something too. After getting in well after midnight the evening before, I'd fallen into bed exhausted, only to toss and turn for hours, sleeping only in fits and starts until I finally gave up on the whole futile process around seven A.M.

"How long until this parade starts, anyway?" I asked, glancing around. We were currently wandering along University Avenue, a broad multilane street that borders the north side of campus and today was serving as part of the parade route.

The place was packed. Happy shouts and laughter came from every direction as people greeted friends or chatted with neighbors. Little kids ran around like escaped circus monkeys, wielding huge wads of sticky cotton candy like sugary weapons. It was impossible to take more than three steps without almost tripping over bikes, baby strollers, or overstimulated dogs twisting their leashes around bystanders' legs. The weather was gorgeous, the mild summer breeze carrying the strong scents of sunscreen, roasted peanuts, and bratwurst. Throngs of eager spectators packed the sidewalks along most of the parade route, staking out their spots with folding lawn chairs and enormous coolers full of cold beverages.

Basically everyone seemed to be having fun except for Bess and me. Oh, and Ned, of course—he'd reluctantly reported for work and was now trailing one of the senior reporters around the parade route. We'd spotted him a few times, and each time he looked more miserable and worried than the last.

I'm not sure if Bess even heard my question. She was staring off into space with a slightly furrowed brow. "What if she chased a bad guy onto a cargo train or something and couldn't get off, and got stuck riding the rails up to, you know, Alaska or somewhere?"

I just shrugged. It wasn't the first time one or the other of us had come up with such an outlandish sequence of events attempting to explain the inexplicable. All morning we'd been trying to come up with a new plan, a new way to proceed. Now that our museum angle had fizzled, we had no idea what to do next. Ned hadn't seen a thing out of the ordinary at the park the previous night, the police had confirmed that Zane Quinn hadn't been anywhere near River

Heights since departing on his vacation, and they were also pretty sure that Marcus Pembleton was as clueless as we were about what had happened to Nancy. There just didn't seem to be any clues at all.

Frankly it made me feel completely helpless. And that's not a feeling I particularly enjoy.

"This is starting to feel like one of those bad true-crime shows on TV," I commented. "Like when some woman in Idaho goes out to put gas in her car or pick up the dry cleaning and is never seen again."

"Don't say that!" Bess looked horrified. "Don't even think it. Nancy's going to be found."

I couldn't help noticing she hadn't said, *We're going to find Nancy.* No wonder. We weren't exactly setting any new land-speed records in mystery solving so far. It was time to face facts—we were nothing without Nancy. At least, that was how it felt. . . .

As we skirted a group of college students dancing around a boom box, I noticed a commotion toward the end of the block. A crowd had gathered on the lawn in front of Mahoney Hall, and more people were running in that direction.

"What's going on over there?" Bess said idly, not really sounding too interested.

I shrugged. "One way to find out."

Leading the way over there, I saw that the gathered crowd consisted mostly of kids under the age of twelve. Even before I pushed my way to the front, I recognized the harsh, commanding voice emanating from the center of the cluster.

"Stay back! I don't want to tell you again!"

Marge Kurz was in the center of the hubbub holding one of her dogs—I couldn't tell if it was Hans or a different one—by a short leash.

"Does he do tricks?" a small, chocolate-smeared boy called out excitedly.

The dog stared at the child, its ears pricked curiously. I winced, remembering the "trick" Kurz's dog had played on me over at Anvil Park.

"No," Kurz yelled angrily at the boy. "Now please leave us alone!"

"This can't be good," I muttered to Bess. "Why would she bring one of those dogs here? Is she nuts?" The woman's dogs seemed hair-trigger under normal circumstances. If the one she was holding decided it needed to protect its mistress from the encroaching children, it would mean certain mayhem.

Bess looked worried too. She cleared her throat and clapped her hands. "Hey, kids!" she called out loudly in her most enthusiastic, cheerful, little-kid-friendly voice. "Listen up. I heard Mo-Mo the Clown is right up the street there at Anvil Park.

You'd better run over there and see him before he thinks nobody likes him and decides to leave!"

"Yay!" most of the little kids cheered, running off immediately in the direction of the park a block or two away. A few still lingered, staring curiously at the dog, but when Kurz glared at them, they scurried after their peers.

"Thanks," Kurz said gruffly, nodding gratefully toward Bess. "Don't know what I would've done if you hadn't come along. Couldn't get the little brats to leave my dog alone."

I bit my tongue, barely resisting the urge to point out how idiotic it was to bring a hypersensitive guard dog to a public parade in the first place. It wasn't worth getting into it at the moment. Instead I said, "By the way, congratulations. Seems your dog busted a break-in at the museum last night."

"You heard about that already, eh?" Kurz's broad face took on a smug expression. "The cops said it was a darn good thing my dog was there to stop that guy. If Klaus hadn't been on the job, that *Chaturanga* display would've been history. So to speak."

She let out a short, eerie, barklike laugh, clearly amused by her own joke. Bess and I exchanged a quick glance. It appeared that the dog trainer hadn't heard about our part in the whole escapade. It figures, I thought. She probably thinks the creature dialed 911 on its own.

"So that dog's name is Klaus?" I said. "The museum staff has been calling him Killer."

Kurz looked oddly pleased by that bit of news. "They have, eh? Well, I suppose it's no wonder. It's true, I like to say that all of my dogs are silent but deadly. A thief would never know one of my boys was even in the room until he saw the fangs in his face." She chortled, seeming a little too pleased with her own imagery. Perhaps noticing my look of distaste, which was echoed on Bess's face, the woman quickly amended, "The dogs wouldn't actually go for the kill—probably—but whoever they surprise might die of fright!"

This last comment didn't seem much less distasteful than the earlier ones to me. Then again, Marge Kurz struck me as a generally distasteful person, and I didn't want to waste any more time making small talk with her. I was impatient to move on, to continue with our investigation. Bess might not believe anymore that we were going to find Nancy, but that only made me all the more determined to keep trying. Which just goes to show, perhaps, that all the optimism in the world can't hold a candle to sheer, unadulterated stubbornness.

Before I could figure out a way to make a more-or-less courteous escape, Kurz checked her watch. "I have to go." She abruptly yanked at her dog's leash, then turned on her heel and strode off without another word to us.

Bess watched the dog trainer and her canine charge weave their way through the crowd until they disappeared from sight. "Charming lady," she said with a sigh. That was about as close as Bess ever came to sarcasm.

We turned and wandered off in the opposite direction. "Let's duck off this main street for a few minutes, okay?" I suggested. "I can't even hear myself think. We need to get away from this crowd for a while, get some air."

"Are you sure?" Bess said. "It sounds like the parade's starting."

I cocked my head and listened. Over the noise of competing boom boxes and shrieking children, I detected the distant sound of a brass band blaring out a familiar patriotic march.

"Sounds that way," I agreed. "But are you really in the mood to stand around and watch a parade right now?"

Bess pursed her lips. "Okay, good point," she said. "Let's go."

In the relative quiet of the side streets a block or

two away from the marchers' route, we forgot about the parade, Marge Kurz, and everything else, to return to the only topic of the slightest interest to either of us: Nancy.

"It's been more than three days now," Bess fretted. "Wherever she is, I just hope she's okay."

I nodded, not really wanting to think about that too much. "So what's our next move here, anyway? I feel like we're wasting time saying the same stuff over and over."

"I don't know." Bess spread her arms helplessly as she walked. "It really just seems like there has to be something we're missing. Some clue, some idea, something someone said . . ."

"I know." I sighed with frustration as I quickly ran over our sparse collection of possible clues for what felt like the millionth time. "All I know is, Nancy would've found herself six times over by now. Are we the world's biggest losers, or what?"

"Don't say that. After all, the police and Mr. Drew haven't had any luck finding her either," Bess pointed out with a ghost of her usual silver-lining-seeking self. She smiled wanly. "And at least we solved one mystery last night, right? Nancy would be proud of us for that one."

"Even though we sort of stumbled onto it accidentally," I said, adding my usual dose of realism to

Bess's sunny-side up attitude. "And even though, according to Krazy Kurz, ol' Klaus could have wrapped up that little attempted burglary all by himself."

Bess giggled. "Yeah, that woman is really something, isn't she?" she said. "I didn't have the heart to tell her those dogs of hers aren't quite as 'silent and deadly' as she thinks. Remember how much noise that dog was making inside the museum?"

"Yeah." I paused, thinking about that. "You know, now that you mention it, it *is* kind of weird."

"What is?"

"That one dog could make that much noise. I mean, he was thumping around in there almost every time I made my rounds."

"I could even hear it from our hiding place," Bess added with a nod. "Once you mentioned it, I started noticing it more and more."

I stopped short and turned to face her. "So we both assumed it was the dog making those noises," I said. "But what if it wasn't?"

"You mean you think someone else might have been inside the museum last night?" Bess looked dubious. "I suppose it's possible. But why?"

My eyes widened. "Because someone else is after that valuable old chess set too!" I exclaimed, suddenly flashing back to something I'd heard but not really thought about the night before. "Marcus Pembleton even hinted at that, remember? He said something about how if he didn't take it, somebody else would. I think."

Bess gasped. "You're right! I'd totally forgotten about that." Then she shook her head. "But wait," she added. "Even if someone else wanted to steal it, how were they planning to get past Killer Klaus?"

"Oh. I almost forgot about that." I shrugged, suddenly realizing we were just half a block from the museum at the moment. "But we might as well check it out. What do we have to lose?"

A tiny smile flitted across her face. "This isn't just your way of making sure we miss seeing Deirdre's float, is it?" she joked.

I rolled my eyes. "All the more reason," I said, noticing that the sounds of the marching bands were getting closer. The parade would probably be reaching University Avenue in the next few minutes. "Come on!"

It only took a few minutes to reach the museum, which looked as silent and empty as it had the day before. We crossed the small parking lot and looked up at the building. As we stood there, we heard a muffled thump and clank from somewhere inside.

"Listen," I said. "There it is again."

"Could it be a broken pipe or something?" Bess asked uncertainly. "It *is* an old building. . . ."

I shrugged. "Let's see if we can hear better from the back."

I led the way around the side of the building. The noises continued sporadically. *Clank. Thump. Bump.*

"Doesn't really sound like a pipe to me," I commented. "It's too—"

I cut myself off with a gasp as we rounded the corner of the building. Marge Kurz was scooting out the back door with a bulging backpack slung over one shoulder!

14

Crashing the Parade

Bess

Hey!" George blurted out loudly. "Stop!"

Ms. Kurz saw us and took off at top speed. Without stopping to think about what we were doing, George and I followed.

I was surprised when our quarry suddenly reversed direction, sprinting back toward the door she'd just left. I slowed almost to a stop, confused. Was she going to try to hide out inside the museum?

A second later I figured it out. Ms. Kurz swung the door wide open, revealing the snarling face of Klaus the guard dog!

"Go on, baby!" Ms. Kurz shouted at the dog. "Get them!"

The dog whined uncertainly, looking up at her. It took a step out the door and then stopped.

147

"Aargh!" she cried. "Useless beast . . ." With that, she spun and sprinted off again.

"Hold it!" George yelped, running after the woman. "You might as well stop—we already saw you!"

The woman ignored her, racing across the yard toward the street. She was still clutching the backpack tightly against herself as she pushed her way through the hedge separating the museum grounds from the sidewalk.

"Come on, let's get her," George cried. I nodded, and we both sped up, dodging the dog, which had trotted out of the doorway and stood staring after its owner. Just as we passed him, Klaus let out a loud bark.

I almost had a heart attack right then and there. Luckily, though, the dog paid no attention to George and me at all. Instead Klaus bounded after his owner, barking happily.

"Follow that dog!" George cried breathlessly.

I followed as she pushed her way through the hedge. The prickly branches caught on my clothes and in my hair, but I ignored them.

Now that I was on the other side of the hedge, I saw that Ms. Kurz was already across the street and halfway through the garden in front of another university building. Klaus was bouncing around underfoot, still barking.

"Get away from me!" the woman shouted at the dog. "Scat! Go on!"

George and I put on a burst of speed, gaining ground on the woman as she took a shortcut across another shady university lawn. "Where's she going?" I panted. "If she keeps heading that way, she's going to run straight into—"

"The parade," George finished succinctly.

By now the sounds of marching bands and cheering spectators were getting loud, indicating that the parade had reached University Avenue. I realized that Ms. Kurz must be heading that way to try to lose herself in the crowd.

Sure enough, when we emerged onto the sidewalk along the avenue a moment later, we saw nothing but a shifting mass of people in front of us. Staring around frantically, I saw a cluster of teen boys, a trio of middle-aged women wearing matching bowling shirts, even my dentist with his wife and kids. But there was no sign of Ms. Kurz.

"There!" George suddenly pointed off to the right. "Check it out—it's Klaus! She must be over there!"

I heard an eager bark. Turning, I saw the guard dog loping along through the crowd as people scattered before him. He was still following his mistress, who was pushing and shoving her way toward the street. As I watched, she darted out into the street and disappeared between a couple of floats.

"Come on!" I said, taking off after her with George at my heels.

By the time we reached the floats, Ms. Kurz was nowhere in sight. I was staring frantically into the crowd on the other side of the street, searching for a glimpse of her reddish hair or unattractive peach velour T-shirt, when I heard the scream of a terrified horse from somewhere nearby.

"Up there!" George cried, pointing beyond the float just ahead of us. The next group in the parade was a small formation of horseback riders wearing old-fashioned cavalry gear.

At the moment, several of the horses were pitching and rearing, their eyes rolling back in their heads with terror as they tried to avoid the dog charging through their midst. Klaus was paying no attention to the frightened animals as he made a beeline for Ms. Kurz, who was scurrying along in the narrow empty alley between the spectators and the parade.

By this time some of the people along the sidelines seemed to be figuring out that something strange was happening. As the cavalry horses broke formation and tried to escape in any direction they could, a few of the spectators pointed at them, the dog, and Ms. Kurz.

"Get her!" George shouted at them at the top of

her lungs, though it was barely enough to make a dent in all the noise. Between the snorting and whinnying horses, their shouting riders, the barking dog, and the normal noises of the parade, I could barely hear her even from just a few feet away. "The redhead with the backpack! Stop her! She's a thief!"

If any of the spectators heard her, they gave no indication of it. Ms. Kurz dashed ahead into the next group in the parade, the River Heights High School marching band. Once again, Klaus followed. As the young musicians saw the dog bounding toward them, they stopped playing in midsong, scattering in all directions. The flag twirlers and cheerleaders, noticing that their music had stopped, turned to see what was happening. As Ms. Kurz dashed through and Klaus leaped toward them, they started shrieking in terror. One girl, braver than the others, paused and threw her pom-poms at the dog before diving for safety with the others.

Klaus paid no attention to any of it, though he did slow down a little as he passed the kid dressed in the costume of the school's mascot, a wildcat. The hapless mascot stood frozen with terror as Klaus sniffed curiously at his or her dangling tail before continuing his pursuit.

George and I were still moving too, trying to catch up. But it wasn't easy—the sudden interruption of Ms. Kurz and her dog had thrown the entire parade into chaos, and we found ourselves having to dodge and weave to make our way through.

"Have . . . to . . . catch . . . her . . . ," George panted as we pushed past a couple of sobbing clarinetists and a white-faced kid with a tuba.

"There are more floats up ahead," I called back, peering at my cousin around the tuba. "It'll be easier up there."

When we finally made it past the high-school marchers, we found ourselves facing the back of an enormous float. I immediately recognized it as the Rackham Industries extravaganza we'd seen at the warehouse the previous day.

"Thank you . . ." An amplified voice floated out over the crowd. "Thank you so much."

"Deirdre," George muttered, glancing upward.

Sure enough, when I looked up I could see that Deirdre was standing in front of the computer-chip throne at the center of the float. She was holding a bouquet of red, white, and blue flowers and wearing a glittering, jewel-encrusted golden tiara. There was a microphone on a stand set up in front of her, and she was speaking into it while waving to the crowd. Biff and a couple of other young men were standing behind the throne dressed in tuxedos.

But I was much less interested in Deirdre and her

escorts than in Marge Kurz. Where had she gone? For a moment I was afraid we'd lost her once and for all. I scanned the crowd on either side of the street and saw no sign of either her or Klaus.

Then I heard a loud bark from somewhere close by. "There!" George exclaimed, pointing off toward the right side of the float.

I looked and saw Ms. Kurz clambering up the side, clutching at the draping garlands of peacock feathers for a handhold. As she finally reached the top and flung her legs over, she kicked one of the flowerpots, sending it crashing over the edge. I winced as it crashed against the pavement, narrowly missing a small boy at the edge of the crowd.

"Hey!" Deirdre exclaimed, finally noticing that something was going on as she spotted the dog trainer climbing to her feet nearby. "What are you doing? Get off my—aaaaah!"

She screamed loudly as Klaus made a flying leap up onto the float, scrabbling to keep on all four feet upon landing. He skidded across the slick golden-colored tiles that formed the floor and crashed into Deirdre's legs, sending her tumbling backward. Her bouquet and her crown both went flying, and she squealed loudly as she narrowly missed bonking her carefully coiffed head on the edge of her throne.

I stared openmouthed at the ridiculous scene until

I realized that George was already dashing forward. "Come on!" she shouted at me over her shoulder.

Soon the two of us were climbing onto the float. By the time I hauled myself up over the edge, Deirdre was on her feet again. Her Miss Rackham Industries sash was askew, and her expression was furious.

"What's going on?" she shouted, glaring from me to her confused-looking escorts to Ms. Kurz, who was trying to step around her excited dog to get to the other side of the float. "This is an outrage! I demand an explanation, or my father will—"

Ignoring her, George reached for her microphone. "Help!" she shouted into it, her words amplified and bouncing out loudly over the surrounding area, where they echoed back at us from the walls of nearby buildings. "Police! We need some police backup, stat!" She suddenly took a step toward the edge, peering into the crowd. "Hey, Ned, is that you? Get up here!"

It was lucky she'd spotted Ned in the crowd. He hoisted himself up over the edge of the float just as Ms. Kurz finally disentangled herself from Klaus and made a run for it. Looking confused, Ned started to step aside.

"No!" George and I screamed at the same time. "Get her!"

Comprehension dawned on Ned's face, and he

stepped back in front of the woman. "Excuse me," he said. At least, that's what it looked like he said—in all the din, I couldn't hear him even though he was only a couple of yards away.

He put a hand out to stop her. Snarling, she swung a fist at him. But Ned was quicker than she was, grabbing her firmly by the wrist to stop the blow.

"Don't let go!" George yelled at him. "Hold on to her, Ned!"

Deirdre had taken back the microphone and was shrieking angrily into it. But none of us were paying attention to her. We were too busy watching as dozens of police officers and firefighters, who had all left their own spots in the parade, started swarming around the float.

Ten minutes later Ms. Kurz was being officially taken into custody by a very confused-looking Chief McGinnis. One of his officers had Klaus safely contained on a leash, where the dog seemed content to heel calmly at his side. The parade was still in chaos, so the chief gestured for all of us—me, George, Ned, and the other officers—to follow him down a side street to a quieter spot.

Soon we were all gathered on the sidewalk in front of Mahoney Hall. Ms. Kurz was swearing and making vague threats at all of us, especially the police. "How dare you!" she shouted hoarsely. "Release me at once! If you don't let me go, I'll sue you right down to your badges for false arrest. . . ."

"All right, settle down, madam," the chief said sternly. "At the very least, I'm going to have to charge you with disruption of the peace." He glanced over at George, Ned, and me. "Although if that's all we're looking at here, you won't be the only one charged," he muttered.

"Open her backpack, Chief," George spoke up. She gestured at the pack, which was sitting at the woman's feet.

I held my breath as the chief nodded at a young officer, indicating for him to do as George had said. If all the police found inside that pack was a bag of dog treats for Klaus, we could be in a lot of trouble.

My fears were assuaged a moment later as the young officer's eyes widened. "Better have a look at this, Chief," he said, holding out the pack.

"What is it?" George asked eagerly.

"I didn't do it!" Ms. Kurz shouted suddenly. "I was framed! There are people in this town who hate me; it's not my fault. I can explain. . . ."

"That's quite enough," Chief McGinnis said with a frown. He reached into the pack and gingerly pulled out an odd-looking piece of wood and a small matching box. "If this is what I think it is, you're going to have quite a bit of explaining to do down at HQ."

I gasped. "Is that . . ."

"The old chess set," George confirmed eagerly. "It's got to be!"

"And that's not all," the chief said, peering into the bag. "There's some antique silver in here too, and what looks to be a few volumes from the Granger Rare Books Collection."

Ms. Kurz continued to profess her innocence for a moment, but then I guess she realized it was hopeless. It was as if a switch inside her head flipped all of a sudden. "All right, you got me," she spat out, her eyes flashing hatred as she glared around at all of us. Nearby, Klaus sat up and let out a low, anxious growl as he watched her. "I was stupid this time, and you got me."

"This time?" George repeated curiously.

"I'll do the questioning, if you don't mind, Miss Fayne," the chief said firmly. He glanced at Ms. Kurz. "This time?"

"You think this is my first time at this?" The woman sneered. "No way! I've been doing this for years, and I've never been caught."

After that the whole story poured out of her quickly. It was almost as if she'd been waiting for a chance to brag about her own cleverness. She had heard about the ancient chess set soon after her recent arrival in River Heights. She had realized immediately just how valuable it could be to certain black-market sources. It turned out that she was in town to rob the museum anyway, planning to make off with the antique silver pieces and rare books the police had just found in her backpack. She'd successfully pulled similar heists a number of times before in other parts of the country. She would move into town and make a big show of getting her business established by loaning out her dogs. Then she would use the information, access, and trust she'd gained to get at the items she wanted, though she never took anything during the time her dogs were actually on guard to avoid drawing suspicion.

When she'd heard about the chess set, though, she hadn't been able to resist adding it to her list. Even though she knew it would be a risk to steal something one of her dogs was actually guarding at the time, she didn't have much choice, since the exhibit would be in town for such a limited amount of time. And it was a risk she was willing to take—the chess set was far more valuable than anything she'd ever taken before. She planned to grab it and the other items while the parade was going on, then feed poisoned meat to Klaus to throw suspicion off herself.

I gasped out loud when she got to that part. "You were going to—to kill your own dog?" I cried. I glanced over at Klaus, who had settled down again. He wasn't exactly the kind of dog I wanted to take home and cuddle with, but that didn't mean I wanted to see him dead.

Ms. Kurz just shrugged. "Dogs are replaceable," she said shortly.

"So what happened?" Chief McGinnis was listening carefully with his arms crossed over his chest. "Should we expect Fido here to keel over? Do we need to call a vet?"

"I didn't have a chance to feed him the poison." Ms. Kurz nodded toward the backpack. "It's still in there—side pocket." She sighed. "That was my second mistake," she declared. "I got spooked. Heard some funny noises inside the museum and was afraid someone was on to me." She glared at us. "I guess that was you clanking around in there, huh?"

"No," George said blankly. "We heard that too. But we thought it was you. Well, actually at first we thought it was Klaus."

"Never!" Ms. Kurz looked more insulted at that accusation than she had at being arrested. "My dogs are carefully trained to avoid such things. Klaus never makes a peep until he confronts an intruder and starts barking."

I gasped and stared at George and Ned. They stared back, their faces immediately going white. I had a feeling we'd all just simultaneously gotten the world's biggest hunch.

"Nancy!" we all shouted at once.

Before a surprised Chief McGinnis could react, we took off at top speed, heading for the museum. Moments later we were rushing through the back door, which was still standing open from Ms. Kurz's earlier escape.

"Nancy! Nancy! Are you in here?" I shouted as loudly as I could. My friends' voices echoed down the halls as they called out as well.

A sudden banging answered our calls. "That way!" Ned cried, pointing forward.

We raced down the hall and emerged into a stairwell. The banging sounds were drifting upward from the floor below . . . along with a muffled cry for help.

"Down here!" George shouted, already leaping for the stairs.

We clattered down to the bottom floor, following the noises to a metal door marked PANTRY. It was bolted shut, but it took Ned only a second to shoot the dead bolt open.

He yanked at the door. It swung open. . . .

"Boy, am I glad to see you!" Nancy greeted us with a weary smile.

15

All's Well That Ends Well

Nancy

Check it out, Nancy," George whispered eagerly. "Deirdre's giving us the evil eye again."

I cracked open one eye to see for myself, shading it against the midday sun reflecting off the water of the country club pool. Sure enough, Deirdre was glaring at me and my friends from her spot across the pool. In fact, she looked even grumpier than usual, which I suspected had less to do with our intrusion into her precious country club than with her very public humiliation the day before at the parade. My friends had filled me in on the whole story—including the part they'd only heard about secondhand, where she'd ripped the seam of her dress stomping around angrily and thereby wound up accidentally showing her underpants to half the town.

"Too bad," I said lazily. "She can shoot me dirty looks all she wants; I'm not budging. Mrs. Abernathy invited us, and she's just as much a member as Deirdre's family." I wriggled, searching for a more comfortable position on the towel-lined teak chair. "Besides, after spending three days in the museum pantry, I think I deserve a little fresh air and sunlight, and this is a perfect place to get it."

Bess gazed at me sympathetically. "That's for sure," she agreed, adjusting the tie on her bikini top. "You poor thing—I still can't believe you were trapped in that tiny little pantry room for so long—"

"Never mind," I said, stopping her before she could get rolling. Over the past twenty-four hours, my friends had apologized over and over again for not finding me sooner. "You guys did great. I still can't believe you found me *and* foiled two robbery attempts at the same time!"

I knew my friends were still blaming themselves, thinking they'd been too slow to put things together and find me. But I was proud of them for figuring out as much as they had, considering how little they had to go on.

Ned turned his head, squinting at me from the next lounge chair. "That reminds me," he said. "Are you ever going to fill us in on how all this got started in the first place?"

"Oh, right." I sat up and glanced around at the three of them. "Let's see, where should I start? Okay, well, you guys know how I like to read through all those unsolved-crime reports George helps me find on the Internet?"

They all burst out laughing. I suppose I'm probably the only person around who considers that sort of thing interesting light reading.

"Are you finished?" I asked them with a grin. "Because if you don't want to hear this . . ."

"No, no." George waved a hand to shush the others. "Go on, Nancy. We're listening."

"Okay, well, I'd really just started to suspect there might be something fishy about that guard dog suddenly turning up at the museum right before the chess exhibit arrived. . . ."

I went on to explain the whole thing. I'd noticed a certain pattern in some of the crimes I'd read about over the past couple of years. That's the kind of thing I'm good at—noticing odd coincidences and putting them together so they make sense. And it definitely seemed odd that several unsolved thefts of valuable (and fenceable) artifacts had occurred in the exact same towns where guard dogs had recently been hired for the first time—a fact that was mentioned in passing in several articles about the crimes. It was a thin connection, true, but just weird enough to catch my attention.

In trying to think like a thief, I'd also realized that the commotion of the busy July Fourth parade could be the perfect cover for a theft at the university museum, the home of many valuable River Heights artifacts. That's why I noted it on my calendar, planning to keep a close watch on the place during the parade if I hadn't turned up anything in the meantime.

Once I started making all those connections, naturally I wanted to talk to Marge Kurz myself—to figure out if she might really be a crook. That's why I had Charlie drop me off at the park that morning. I'd heard from several people that Marge Kurz and her dogs had become a regular sight there in the mornings. Unfortunately, that particular morning, I missed her thanks to my car trouble.

Not wanting to waste time, I decided to walk over to the museum and poke around there a little. I'd forgotten that the place was closing early that day, along with the rest of the university, for the holiday weekend. Luckily, though, my friend Zane Quinn was there helping to close up. He was rushing off to make a plane in Chicago, but he agreed to let me in to snoop around a little. He owed me a favor, since Dad had helped him get released from jail early for good behavior, and then I'd recommended him to Mrs. Abernathy for the security job at the museum.

Anyway, since Zane was on his way out, he left me

with a key to the museum so I could let myself out again after hours. But then, while I was snooping around, I heard the door open again. It turned out to be Mrs. Abernathy and Marge Kurz, who was bringing Klaus in for the weekend. I ducked into the pantry when they came by, not wanting them to catch me inside the museum—mostly because I didn't want to get Zane in trouble for letting me in. I guess Mrs. Abernathy must have thrown the dead bolt when she went by, because when I tried to let myself out a little while later, the door wouldn't budge.

By that time the two women had left. Klaus barked the first few times he heard me banging on the door or the water pipes that passed through the pantry. But he lost interest after a while, and no matter how much I banged and shouted, nobody heard me.

Or so I'd thought, anyway, until my friends told me they'd heard me from outside. "I just wish we'd investigated the noises sooner," George commented, drumming her fingers on the arm of her lounge chair. "I mean, how could we think a dog would make that kind of racket? Stupid, stupid, stupid."

"Quit it," I insisted. "You guys did great. How were you supposed to know all that stuff about Marge Kurz and the other thefts? You had nothing to go on but a couple of cryptic notes in my calendar. And even with nothing more than that, you solved the whole case!"

Oh, there was a little more to it than that, of course. Most mysteries are kind of sloppy and sprawling, after all, with a lot of circumstantial offshoots and loose ends. For instance, there was the whole Marcus Pembleton connection. I still wasn't sure how much I'd contributed to his impulsive scheme to steal that chess set. He'd immediately gotten kind of upset when I stopped by his farm on Tuesday afternoon to pick his brain, thinking that there was no one in town likely to know more about that kind of obscure artifact. Since he hadn't been able to tell me much, I called Simone to ask about the next chess club meeting, figuring I could try to do my research there instead. But of course, I never made it.

"What an ordeal," Bess said, shaking her head. "It's just lucky you were trapped in the pantry where there was plenty to eat and drink."

I nodded. "Definitely lucky," I agreed. "Other than worrying about how frantic you all must have been about me—and wondering about the robberies, too—I was pretty comfortable in there. I figured at the very worst, I'd be stuck in there until the museum opened again after the holiday weekend."

George stared at me curiously. "That reminds me," she said. "There's no bathroom in that pantry, right?"

"George!" Bess chided, looking horrified.

I smiled, though I couldn't help blushing a little.

"Yeah, that reminds me, too," I mumbled, indicating the empty glass on the teak table nearby. "I drank my whole iced tea—guess that means I'd better go find that empty pickle jar. . . ."

Shuddering visibly, Bess quickly changed the subject as George and Ned laughed. "Well, it sounds like Ms. Kurz will be going to jail for a good long time," she said brightly. "But the other good news is that Mrs. Abernathy isn't going to press charges against Mr. Pembleton."

Ned grinned. "Yeah, and Mr. P even offered to adopt Kurz's dogs while she's in the slammer. Luckily the police said no. They're going to find them good homes with people who actually know how to handle them."

"That's good." I smiled at them fondly, stretching out on my lounge chair. "See, you guys did good. I guess that means I've taught you well. Not only did you solve a couple of tough crimes, but I know if I ever go missing again, I can count on you to find me."

They all groaned in unison. "Forget it, Nancy Drew," George declared, speaking for all of them. "If you ever go missing again, we're going with you!"

THE HARDY BOYS

BOYS

UNDERCOVER BROTHERS™

They've got motorcycles,
their cases are ripped from the headlines,
and they work for ATAC:
American Teens Against Crime.

CRIMINALS, BEWARE:
THE HARDY BOYS ARE ON YOUR TRAIL!

Starting in **Summer 2005,**
Frank and Joe will begin telling all-new stories of crime,
danger, death-defying stunts, mystery, and teamwork.

Ready? Set? Fire it up!

HAVE YOU READ ALL OF THE ALICE BOOKS?

PHYLLIS REYNOLDS NAYLOR

STARTING WITH ALICE
Atheneum Books for
  Young Readers
  0-689-84395-X
Aladdin Paperbacks
  0-689-84396-8

ALICE IN BLUNDERLAND
Atheneum Books for
  Young Readers
  0-689-84397-6

LOVINGLY ALICE
Atheneum Books for
  Young Readers
  0-689-84399-2

THE AGONY OF ALICE
Atheneum Books for
  Young Readers
  0-689-31143-5
Aladdin Paperbacks
  0-689-81672-3

ALICE IN RAPTURE,
  SORT-OF
Atheneum Books for
  Young Readers
  0-689-31466-3
Aladdin Paperbacks
  0-689-81687-1

RELUCTANTLY ALICE
Atheneum Books for
  Young Readers
  0-689-31681-X
Aladdin Paperbacks
  0-689-81688-X

ALL BUT ALICE
Atheneum Books for
Young Readers
  0-689-31773-5
Aladdin Paperbacks
  0-689-85044-1

ALICE IN APRIL
Atheneum Books for
  Young Readers
  0-689-31805-7
Aladdin Paperbacks
  0-689-81686-3

ALICE IN-BETWEEN
Atheneum Books for
  Young Readers
  0-689-31890-0
Aladdin Paperbacks
  0-689-81685-5

ALICE THE BRAVE
Atheneum Books for
  Young Readers
  0-689-80095-9
Aladdin Paperbacks
  0-689-80598-5

ALICE IN LACE
Atheneum Books for
  Young Readers
  0-689-80358-3
Aladdin Paperbacks
  0-689-80597-7

OUTRAGEOUSLY ALICE
Atheneum Books for
  Young Readers
  0-689-80354-0
Aladdin Paperbacks
  0-689-80596-9

ACHINGLY ALICE
Atheneum Books for
  Young Readers
  0-689-80533-9
Aladdin Paperbacks
  0-689-80595-0
Simon Pulse
  0-689-86396-9

ALICE ON THE OUTSIDE
Atheneum Books for
  Young Readers
  0-689-80359-1
Simon Pulse
  0-689-80594-2

GROOMING OF ALICE
Atheneum Books for
  Young Readers
  0-689-82633-8
Simon Pulse
  0-689-84618-5

ALICE ALONE
Atheneum Books for
  Young Readers
  0-689-82634-6
Simon Pulse
  0-689-85189-8

SIMPLY ALICE
Atheneum Books for
  Young Readers
  0-689-84751-3
Simon Pulse
  0-689-85965-1

PATIENTLY ALICE
Atheneum Books for
  Young Readers
  0-689-82636-2
Simon Pulse
  0-689-87073-6

INCLUDING ALICE
Atheneum Books for
  Young Readers
  0-689-82637-0

From 2-time Newbery Medalist
E. L. Konigsburg

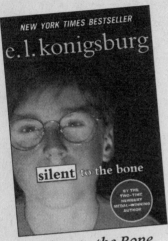

NEW YORK TIMES BESTSELLER

e. l. konigsburg

silent to the bone

BY THE TWO-TIME NEWBERY MEDAL–WINNING AUTHOR

Silent to the Bone
0-689-83602-3

*From the Mixed-up Files of
Mrs. Basil E. Frankweiler*
NEWBERY MEDAL WINNER
0-689-71181-6

The View from Saturday
NEWBERY MEDAL WINNER
0-689-81721-5

*Jennifer, Hecate, Macbeth,
William McKinley, and Me, Elizabeth*
NEWBERY HONOR BOOK
0-689-84625-8

Altogether, One at a Time
0-689-71290-1

The Dragon in the Ghetto Caper
0-689-82328-2

Father's Arcane Daughter
0-689-82680-X

Journey to an 800 Number
0-689-82679-6

*A Proud Taste for Scarlet
and Miniver*
0-689-84624-X

The Second Mrs. Giaconda
0-689-82121-2

Throwing Shadows
0-689-82120-4

Aladdin Paperbacks • Simon & Schuster Children's Publishing
www.SimonSaysKids.com